Boys Life

Sasaki and Miyano

First-Years

NOVELIZATION
Kotoko Hachijo

ORIGINAL STORY & ART
Shou Harusono

YEN ON
New York

Sasaki and Miyano

Novelization: Kotoko Hachijo
Original Story & Art: Shou Harusono

FIRST-
YEARS

Translation by Kevin Steinbach
Cover art by Shou Harusono

NOVEL SASAKI TO MIYANO ICHINENSEI
©Shou Harusono 2020 ©Kotoko Hachijo 2020
First published in Japan in 2020 by KADOKAWA CORPORATION, Tokyo. English translation right arranged with KADOKAWA CORPORATION, Tokyo, through TUTTLE-MORI AGENCY, INC., Tokyo.

English translation © 2023 by Yen Press, LLC

Yen On
150 West 30th Street, 19th Floor
New York, NY 10001

Visit us at yenpress.com
facebook.com/yenpress
twitter.com/yenpress
yenpress.tumblr.com
instagram.com/yenpress

First Yen On Edition: April 2023
Edited by Yen On Editorial: Leilah Labossiere
Designed by Yen Press Design: Liz Parlett

Yen On is an imprint of Yen Press, LLC.
The Yen On name and logo are trademarks of Yen Press, LLC.

Library of Congress Cataloging-in-Publication Data
Names: Hachijo, Kotoko, author. | Harusono, Shou, creator, illustrator. | Steinbach, Kevin, translator.
Title: Sasaki and Miyano : first-years / Kotoko Hachijo ; story/illustration, Shou Harusono ; translation by Kevin Steinbach.
Other titles: Novel Sasaki and Miyano. English
Description: First Yen On edition. | New York, NY : Yen On, 2023.
Identifiers: LCCN 2022051972 | ISBN 9781975352103 (v. 1 ; trade paperback)
Subjects: CYAC: Love—Fiction. | Friendship—Fiction. | Gay people—Fiction. | Schools—Fiction. | LCGFT: Romance fiction. | Gay fiction. | Short stories. | Light novels.
Classification: LCC PZ7.1.H14 Sas 2023 | DDC [Fic]—dc23
LC record available at https://lccn.loc.gov/2022051972

ISBNs: 978-1-9753-5210-3 (paperback)
978-1-9753-5211-0 (ebook)

10 9 8 7 6 5 4 3 2 1

LSC-C

Printed in the United States of America

Sasaki and Miyano

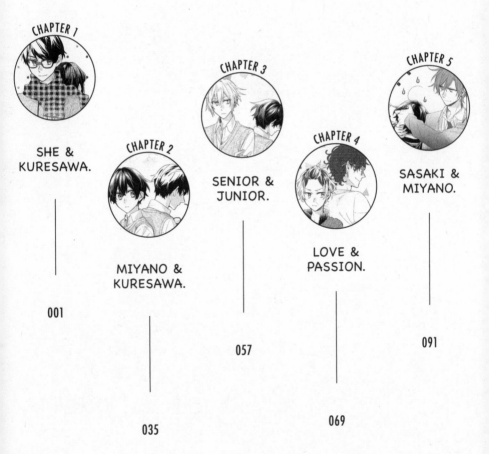

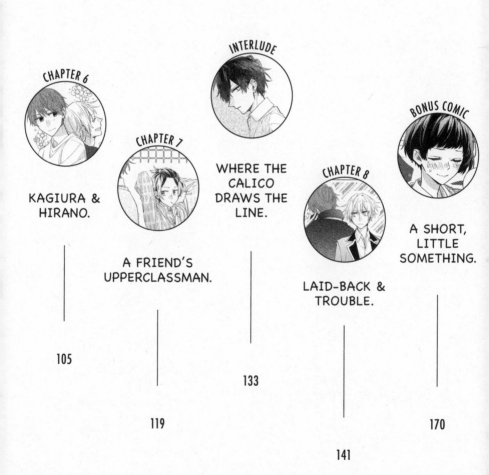

Sasaki and Miyano

CHAPTER 1 · SHE & KURESAWA.

I love the stars. My name is Tasuku Kuresawa, and I've always been entranced by the night sky—by the heavens so filled with specks of light that it feels like nothing else exists between them and human life here on Earth. I knew that one way or another, my future would inevitably revolve around those stars.

My parents encouraged my interest, although they may have been a little worried about the way their son seemed totally obsessed. Still, they felt it was good to have an unwavering passion.

However, despite my certainty, even my little world of a star-filled future could change. Near the end of the rainy season, in my third and final year of middle school, my class went on a trip, but one of our classmates couldn't make it. I tagged along when our group went to visit her in the hospital and encountered a radiance as bright as any star.

"Hee-hee! Nice to meet you, Kuresawa. I'm Yuki Fujimi. I

guess it's odd to say 'nice to meet you,' huh? We've been in class together for so long... Anyway, thanks for coming to see me."

Wow, she sure is cute! I thought.

Our meeting felt like a bolt from the blue. It marked the beginning of my new life with her.

✳✳✳

"First-year students, please begin the procession into the gymnasium," a teacher said. The words, accompanied by the static hiss from the mic, emerged from the open gym and drifted into the sky. The student at the head of the queue started forward, and we all filed into the gym in an untidy line.

Unlike middle school graduation two weeks earlier, here at the high school entrance ceremony, I felt almost floaty, a mix of anticipation and anxiety mingling inside me. The fabric of my new uniform was still stiff, and I had a red artificial flower pinned to my chest. All of it seemed so novel. How could I not be jittery with excitement?

A few minutes ago, we'd assembled in a classroom where we were given some handouts and told how the ceremony would go. I'd taken the opportunity to text my girlfriend a picture—a shot I'd snapped of the courtyard before we all went inside. You could practically hear the hubbub through the screen.

My mind flitted back to her response: It really is all boys! Wish I could see a shot of you, Tasuku. Well, that put me in a tight spot. I guess her request was only natural, since we were dating and all, but I was still a little shy about selfies. I was going to meet my parents after the ceremony was over, and I was sure they'd want to take a commemorative photo. I could just send her that.

I hoped she'd like it.

4

*　　*　　*

Just last week, I started dating my girlfriend, Yuki. We'd been classmates in middle school. When I told her how I felt about her and asked her out on the day of the graduation ceremony—totally cliché, right?—her reaction was, well, less than ideal.

She was often sick and was in and out of the hospital a lot, so I didn't actually see her at school very much. I'd technically been in class with her for months, yet her name was all I'd known about her. If we'd passed each other on the street, I probably wouldn't have recognized her. She was such a rare sight at school that even in our class photo at the beginning of the year, she was just a circle with a name in it. To me, she might as well have been made of thin air.

She and I had been assigned to the same group for the class trip, but the teacher warned us that Yuki probably wouldn't be able to come. We operated on that assumption as our group got ready to go. It hadn't made much difference; we'd talked about what kind of souvenir we should bring her, but that was about it.

I don't remember who suggested we visit her in the hospital. It was someone in our group for the trip, but I don't even know if it was a guy or girl. The idea, though, proved to be a momentous one: My life branched off in an entirely unprecedented direction from that point on.

Yuki had thanked each of the group members, and she'd even remembered my name. "Thanks for coming to see me." She'd said my name cautiously, as if trying to be sure she had it right. "Nice to meet you, Kuresawa." That's what she said. Her bashful tone tickled me.

I guess the other members of my group had all talked to her at least once or twice before. Mine was the only name she was saying for the first time, the syllables new and unfamiliar on her tongue. The sound of it as she tried it out wouldn't leave my mind.

"Did you have fun on the trip, Kuresawa?"

"Oh! The trip. Right. Yeah, I guess." I had been so taken with her that I was hardly thinking about anything else.

"You guess, my foot!" one of my buddies burst out. "We called you, like, fifteen times, and you still wouldn't leave the planetarium!"

"Do you like planetariums?" Yuki asked.

"Uh-huh." Here, she had been kind enough to ask about me, but I couldn't seem to figure out where to go with it. I'd never had this much trouble talking to my other classmates.

As I sputtered, the conversation had moved on without me. People started holding up phones to show off their photo galleries. Yuki didn't seem completely comfortable, which I guess made sense for someone who was so rarely at school, but she still made an effort to talk to everybody. Even me, who couldn't seem to say anything back.

In the end, I'd found myself smitten with her smile, which looked nothing like I had imagined from a girl who was supposed to be frail with illness. I was bewitched by her hair—a deep black as dark as the cosmos—which rippled each time she responded politely to someone. When the sun peeked out from behind the rainy-season clouds, filtered through the hospital windows and lit upon her smile, it shone as radiant as Aldebaran, the brightest star in the Taurus constellation. Her eyes glimmered, lovely as a clear, starlit night, and swallowed me whole.

She had a good head on her shoulders, she was cheerful, and, above all, she was cute! From that day forward, she was all

I could think about. Even when I was thinking about the stars, my mind would wander to her every time.

The seasons changed, and as the nights (when you could observe the stars in the sky!) got longer, my yearning for her grew keener. Aldebaran is especially visible in winter, so every night, when I looked up at the heavens, it was like I saw her smiling back at me.

The problem was that she didn't feel the same way. I was just someone who'd started tagging along to visit her in the hospital, and as far as she was concerned, we hardly had anything in common. As I listened to her chat with other friends, I discovered she was really into manga and TV dramas, but I didn't read many manga and I didn't watch much television, so it was hard for me to be a part of those conversations. My interest in the cosmos was obvious, but those talks threatened to go from conversations to lectures. Still, I figured talking about the stars was better than trying to BS my way through a discussion about something I knew nothing about, so I stuck to chatting about astronomy. It wouldn't have been right to try to make myself the center of attention while she was talking to her friends, so I settled for dropping in little bits of information here and there, like about her star sign or mine. Or I would mention stars she'd likely be able to see out the window of her hospital room.

As time went on, her attitude toward me softened; it no longer seemed to take the wind out of her sails to have me around while she and her friends were chatting. When she was talking about her favorite things, she had a strength and vivacity that could almost make you forget she was hospitalized. At least until visiting hours were over and reality came crashing down.

"Oh... Is it that time already?" she said, and I knew the look of loneliness on her face would never have been there if we'd just been having a long chat after school. It would have been easy. She could have just called home and told them she would be a little late getting back. Or said, "All right, see you at school tomorrow!" But the fact was that she was in the hospital, and that meant there were limits on her fun. Most kids our age had enough problems just dealing with compulsory education. When I thought about how much harder it was for her, I could barely stand it.

I wish she could smile more. I wanted to make her happy. Exactly because she had the strength of heart to stand on her own without even worrying about herself.

The first thing I decided to do was bring her a present: a manga. I'd listened to her talk with her friends enough to have a pretty good idea of what she liked. It wouldn't be too extravagant for a hospital-visit gift, and I could afford it with my allowance. If she didn't like it, that would be good to know, too. I could ask her to tell me what she liked instead.

So for the first time, I went to the hospital by myself, carrying the manga I'd settled on after much agonizing.

"You're alone today?" she asked, surprised.

I nodded. "Do you like this one?" I asked and handed her the book. It was one that had just come out.

"Are you a mind reader?!" she exclaimed, and the way she put her hands to her mouth was so unbearably cute, I couldn't hold back a weird sound. I asked why she seemed so surprised. "Oh," she said, "I thought I must have mentioned it..." Her shy smile was even cuter. It was the same expression she had when she talked with her friends, easy and relaxed. Even though it was just the two of us. It was enough to make me smile, too.

"Do you like this series too, Kuresawa?" she asked.

"Oh, uh, not really. I just thought you might enjoy it."

"Aw, I'm sorry to hear that. But it still makes me happy. Would you like to read it, Kuresawa?"

"Sure. I'd love to know more about which series you like."

Her eyes sparkled at that, and I was thrilled. That was the look I'd hoped to see. A warm glow of happiness bubbled up within me as I listened diligently to her explain the appeal of her favorite manga. They had something to do with...guy friends? In love? I didn't really get it. But I did think she looked adorable as she said, "It just gives you the warm fuzzies!"

There wasn't a cloud in the sky that night. It looked even more beautiful than usual.

There was a constant risk of catching a cold in the winter, so a lot of the time I wasn't able to visit Yuki even though we'd gotten to know each other a little better. Each time I did go, though, she thanked me for the gifts I brought her. The day she finally asked me "Will you tell me about the stars?" I was there until visiting hours ended and they had to kick me out, and my folks really tore into me when I got home.

"When you visit someone in the hospital, they can't just tell you to go away. Not even if you're talking their ear off!" they said, and I took those words to heart. Although Yuki and I had more topics of conversation now, I was still just a classmate who came to visit her sometimes while she was ill. She had plenty of friends who were closer to her than I was.

I'm embarrassed to admit that I'd presumed a lot about what a girl who was sick in the hospital would be like. Worse, when she was released, I was swamped with studying for tests and only found out about it through the grapevine. I didn't even know where she lived. That's how it was for me. There was still such a distance between us.

I knew that, but I still did it. I confessed and asked her to go out with me.

"Why would you tell me that today? Is it because you won't have to live with it if I shoot you down?" Her face was bright red. I was sure that due to radiative cooling—the loss of body heat—the chilly air must be virtually toxic to her. I knew the blush in her cheeks wasn't because of my request—she looked at me not with joy or even embarrassment but with disbelief.

"No, it's because this graduation ceremony is the only time you've come to school recently. I never had a chance to ask you. I don't know your address or your cell number. I heard you got out of the hospital, but you haven't been to school once since then. Heck, you have a fever right now, don't you?"

"Yeah, a slight one… You're right. I see what you mean!" She laughed aloud. I'd been expecting this, but it wasn't a very promising reaction.

I was annoyed to notice we were attracting stares. I guess a guy and a girl standing and talking to each other in the hallway while everybody else was busy taking pictures with their class-mates stood out. I could feel their gazes prickling my skin.

Her slim fingers gripped the tube containing her diploma. Her nails were perfectly shaped. That was just one of countless small details I noticed about her as I took a deep breath. I knew that if I didn't do something, I would regret it, maybe forever.

"I know you probably can't answer me right this second," I said. "I know we don't know each other that well. I think all I've done by asking today is horrify you. But maybe you could give me a chance."

"What kind of chance?" she asked. The way she cocked her head was adorable, which made me panic a little. If I didn't make the most of this opportunity, someone else would snatch her away before I could blink.

"Let me see you again. Can I come see you?"

"I'm out of the hospital."

"Right, and I want to see you when you're healthy, too!"

She laughed again at how sure I sounded, and then, with a touch of bashfulness, she told me her address.

"I really like you," I reiterated. She just looked at the ground. Even the way her long hair brushed her cheeks was adorable. I couldn't care less if people were staring at us anymore.

"Y-yes. I see that now."

"If you… If you'll go out with me, I'll tell you how much I care about you every day!" I said.

"That's too much!"

"It's the truth."

She shrugged me off with a half-exasperated "Sure, I hear you!" I saw her to the nurse's office, then went back to my classroom, still wishing I could have done more.

Her family took her to the hospital, where she ended up being admitted again after some tests. So, starting the next day, I visited her in her sickroom several times.

She finally gave me her answer in March, on the day she left the hospital again.

✳✳✳

I learned that sometimes she was only in the hospital for a week at a time, but often it was a month or more. Even when she looked healthy, she told me, she could become ill suddenly, and it could drag on as she struggled to recover. Her problem was something respiratory, but it manifested as a wide range of symptoms and didn't have a specific diagnosis. I hadn't realized how common it was for someone to be sick without being diagnosed with a specific condition. She told me that her rule of thumb was "Just try not to catch a cold," and bearing that in mind, I took every precaution to be sure I didn't get her sick.

She attended an online high school whenever her health allowed, and I figured the fact that she was able to go to school in any form meant her physical strength was doing better than it had been in middle school.

Things are never that simple, though, and she was back in the hospital as summer began.

Midterms were at the end of May, after the Golden Week holiday. My schedule was so haphazard that Yuki and I spent a lot of time texting each other when we weren't able to meet in person; when I sent her a message saying I would come see her and she replied, You need to focus on your tests, Tasuku. I couldn't really argue. Instead, we promised to talk in the evenings—only for a short while, though. I would go out on the veranda and look at the sky in the direction of the hospital and listen to her voice, so soft, it was almost a whisper.

"Can you see it? The summer triangle?" I asked. The constellation Cygnus was featured in one of her favorite series, and she wanted to know which one it was. I heard her grunt slightly over the phone, no doubt squinting to try to make out the sky.

"I see lots of stars, but I don't know which is which," she finally said.

"I wish I was with you. I could point it out." It was awfully hard to tell what she was looking at just over the phone.

"Guess what. I looked for it yesterday, too. But I couldn't find it. I thought maybe taking a photo would make it easier for you to tell me which one it was..."

"Mm-hm."

"But it didn't come out at all!" she groaned. It wasn't like her to sound so frustrated.

"Yeah, I know. Smartphones aren't the best for getting pictures of the stars. Believe me, I've tried."

She chuckled, the sound of her voice tickling my ear. It was such a bittersweet moment; I couldn't help laughing, too. It made me feel better that we could spend time like this, even if we couldn't physically be together. I really wished I could hold her in my arms, but this was enough for now. I fell more and more in love with her every day.

The moment I tried to channel the feelings welling up in my heart into the words "I love you," though, there was a coughing fit on the other end of the phone. "Are you okay?" I asked. "Don't make yourself worse. Close the window, and make sure you're dressing warm."

"You're such a worrier!"

"Well, yeah. You're my girlfriend."

I talked to my classmates sometimes about having a girlfriend, but I deliberately tried not to use the word too much with her. It was almost like saying those three special words but a little different... It could be kind of embarrassing. Without quite realizing it, I think my nerves had gotten into my voice. She was feeling the same way; she made a sound that wasn't quite an acknowledgment and wasn't quite a laugh and finally just said, "Yeah." I could easily imagine her nodding.

"Next time you're out of the hospital, let's go to the planetarium together. I'll show you where the stars are."

"Yeah. That sounds like fun. Good luck with your studying," she said.

Twice a week, we shared these evening conversations. They were always too short, but I found them encouraging. They motivated me to focus on my work so that I wouldn't embarrass her by totally bombing my exams. I wasn't sending her as many text messages these days, to convey how seriously I was studying with exams looming. Instead, I took comfort in thinking about the day when I would be able to see her again.

On the afternoon of the last day of exams, I was finally able to go visit her. I was shocked to discover that her hair was short! Her long, beautiful hair now barely reached her ears.

"Huh?" I said, freezing the moment I opened the sliding door. I'd seen something like this on the news—they'd talked about how some illnesses made your hair fall out, or how a patient's hair might be cut before surgery so it wouldn't be in the way. Her mysterious illness—could it be that while I hadn't been able to see her, they'd figured out what it was? My heart started pounding, and an unpleasant bead of sweat ran down my back. I was filled with a consuming anxiety that gnawed away at me. I gently closed the door, and finally I managed, "Is it okay if I ask?"

"Hmm? Ask what? Aren't you going to sit? Here, set your bag down. It must be heavy."

"What happened to your hair?"

"I cut it. There's a barbershop on the first floor of the hospital."

Her voice was so light and cheerful, I was almost swept

away by the sound of it. But I forced myself to stay focused. "Is that all? There's no, like, reason?"

"I just felt like a new look. Surprised?" She didn't appear to be or sound like she was hiding anything.

Nearly collapsing with relief, I looked out the window, which I noticed was still open. Or at least, I pretended to look, but mostly I was trying to calm my spiking heart rate.

"Don't do that," I said.

"What? Don't you like girls with short hair?" she asked. It wasn't how she usually talked—I guess she'd been hoping for a better reaction from me. Fair enough, after all the times I'd exclaimed about how cute she was just because she'd put on a new color of lipstick. So much so that she finally said, "Enough already!" although it was with a smile. Personally, I never felt it was enough.

After a moment, I said, "You could even shave your head. As long as you're still alive. You look really cute." I wished I could have just burst out that her hair looked great. It did—it made her silhouette even more distinctive than when she'd had long hair.

"Hee-hee! Hee-hee-hee..."

"Aw, why you gotta laugh like that...?" She was genuinely bashful, and it twisted me into knots, too. She was so unbelievably lovely, I felt shy just meeting her eyes.

Oh, I see. That's really all there is to it. When I caught on to her embarrassment, I finally started to feel my anxiety ebb away. I almost slumped into the visitor's chair. "Hey, change of subject," I said. "I'm going to take the Star Test in August."

"Star Test?"

The Astrology Certification Association's Star Test was a knowledge exam for laypeople. It was offered twice a year, in

March and August, and tested general knowledge about space and astronomy. I'd been busy with school tests in March, but the August exam would fall during summer break, and I wanted to try my hand at it.

I adored everything about stars and the cosmos. I'd even chosen a high school with an Astronomy Club, and I hoped to study the subject in college. The origin of my passion could be found far back in my childhood. My parents had taken me on a trip to Iwate Prefecture, north of Tokyo, where we'd visited Kenji Miyazawa Fairy Tale Village, a theme park with areas based on children's stories by the famous author Kenji Miyazawa. It was a dream come true for a small child.

I was especially taken with one corner that was all about the stars. I was too young to go walking around at night, so this was my first exposure to that world of mystery. It seemed like a place of wonder I shouldn't have been able to experience until I was old enough to go out on my own after darkness fell. I knew about the moon and the stars from picture books, of course, but in my books, they all had faces, nothing like the real heavenly bodies that shone in the night sky.

That was what first prompted my interest in the stars, and seeing *Night on the Galactic Railroad*, a movie that was based on one of Miyazawa's stories, further stoked my infatuation. It seemed only natural that I should want to find a job that had something to do with the stars.

Unlike some other exams, the Star Test didn't actually certify you for anything; it was just for hobbyists. You could say that made it impractical, but I was hungry for every opportunity to learn before I got to college, and this would make a good benchmark to see how I was doing.

I wanted to spend as much of June and July as I could

studying for it. I had to prepare for finals too, of course. And even though the Astronomy Club only met once a week, there was a mountain of things I wanted to do. It meant I might not be able to visit Yuki as often, so it was with some trepidation that I brought up the subject, but she promptly replied, "Don't worry about coming here, then, Tasuku. Work hard!"

✳✳✳

Since I had some leeway until around the middle of June, I was able to keep visiting her once or twice a week. The end of the month was approaching, though, and final exams with it, so I had to stop going. Even when I had a free moment, she sometimes turned me down. My parents are here today, she'd say, or I've got lots of schoolwork to do.

A hospital room is basically a patient's living space, and she treated it like her home; she felt that if someone came to visit her, she had to entertain them. I knew I couldn't intrude when she had told me exactly why we couldn't meet, so I fought down my burning desire to see her and contented myself with a text message or two before hitting the books again. She didn't get back to me until late—she must have been really busy.

The day of finals came at last, and afterward, I was able to go see Yuki for the first time in almost two weeks. In the lobby's hallway, I bumped into her mother.

"Hello, Ms. Fujimi," I said, dipping my head in a polite greeting. We'd met each other before but always in Yuki's room. Never alone like this. Anyone would have a case of nerves upon suddenly encountering their girlfriend's mother.

The woman in front of me looked very much like her

daughter, although without the worrying thinness. Sometimes when I saw her, I almost had the impression that I was seeing how Yuki would look when she was healthy.

"Oh, Kuresawa. You came," Ms. Fujimi said.

"Yes, ma'am. I haven't had a lot of chances recently. I'm sorry for that."

She motioned me down the hallway. We went to a lounge area on the far side of the floor—a carpeted space with a few sofas, some vending machines, and little bookshelves. A window framed a lovely view of a small green space with a playground for young patients.

"It's all right. I'm sure you must be busy."

"It could be worse. Yuki must have it rougher than I do. She sounds just about snowed under with schoolwork. Do you think everything's going okay?"

"Yes...I should think so. I'm sorry; I really don't know for certain."

The way she said that felt strange. Why? Yuki said her parents came at least once every couple of days to collect her laundry. And since she was going to a correspondence school, her parents would have to be involved in submitting her homework by mail. It didn't make sense.

"I'm sorry, but what do you mean you don't know? Come to think of it, Yuki mentioned that her extended family was coming last week. They all live far away, right? They were supposedly in town for something else."

Without really meaning it to, my voice was getting harder and harder. I couldn't shake the sense that Yuki's mom had let something very important slip. I knew this wasn't the way to behave with my girlfriend's mother, but a very not-calm emotion was flooding my chest at that moment.

"I'm sorry. That text last week... My daughter didn't send it. I did," Ms. Fujimi said awkwardly.

The words I was about to say abandoned me. "Really?" I choked. I couldn't come up with anything else.

"Yuki caught a cold. It was nothing serious, but the fever wouldn't go down. You're busy studying to make your dreams come true, aren't you, Kuresawa? It would be such a shame if you were too worried about her to focus on your work. I talked to her about it, and she agreed."

The words were kind, thoughtful, but they cut me to the quick. In short, she was still treating me like an outsider in all this—saying the right things but using them to keep me at arm's length. When Yuki was at her lowest, that was exactly when I wanted to be there for her, but I hadn't even been told that she wasn't feeling well.

A chill went through me and my vision seemed to swim. I said quietly, "If Yuki had died and you had never even told me, I would never have forgiven you for as long as I'd lived." I wasn't shouting, but I was as firm as I could be. I didn't have a chance, however, to see how Yuki's mother reacted.

"Tasuku!" Yuki herself called out before our conversation could go any further. She was wearing a thin cardigan over her hospital gown and was staring at me wide-eyed. She stood straight, walking so steadily, you would never have guessed she was dangerously ill.

"Wait... I thought you had a fever," I said.

She looked from me to her mother and back, as confused as I was angry. "That was last week. I'm fine now. But, Tasuku, about what you just said..." She sounded conciliatory. But I realized: *She knew. She knew her mother was pushing me away.* The revelation made my breath catch in my throat.

Maybe I should have figured it out sooner. You could see it in our chat history. She'd even encouraged me not to visit as often, hadn't she? If she *hadn't* been in on that lie, she could've told me during one of our conversations that her mom had sent the text without her consent.

"You heard that? Do you get what I'm saying, then?"

"I didn't want you to worry," she said slowly. "It was just a cold."

So I was right, I realized with a rush of disappointment. If she'd overheard my argument with her mother and still thought this way, then there was no point. She didn't understand my feelings. If something happened, I would just be left out of the loop again.

"I'd like to talk. Can we go to your room? Or are you in the middle of something?" I asked.

"No, nothing in particular. I was just checking on Mom since she hadn't come back." She glanced at her mother.

"Take your time. Have a good, long talk," her mom said. I felt my cheeks flush. I'd been mistaken that she was forcing us apart. It was Yuki and I who failed to understand each other. We were supposed to be dating, but it seemed like we weren't on the same page.

I squeezed out the words "Let's go," but they were much quieter than I'd meant them to be. I swallowed hard, a bitter taste in my mouth, the truth of the matter weighing me down.

"I told you, the test doesn't give any special qualifications or anything. I just wanted to see if I could do it. It's not so important that I would set everything else aside to study for it."

Yuki was sitting nonchalantly on her bed. I could see her in my peripheral from where I sat on a small sofa in a corner of the room—it was where her mother often sat. I was deliberately trying to keep myself at an angle to her, afraid that if I faced her head-on, I would only get angry.

"But you had finals, too," she pointed out.

"Yeah, but those are about stuff I've already learned. I've been studying the topics all along. I wasn't trying to cram. One visit a week wouldn't have hurt."

"Fine, but... Really, it was only a cold."

"With a fever that didn't go down for days, right? What would you have done if it had gotten worse?" The thought of my girlfriend tormented by vomiting and rashes made my heart sink in my chest. We hadn't been dating very long, but it was enough time for me to have gotten glimpses of how hard it was on her when she was feeling sick. I thought of how helpless and lost I felt each time she finally couldn't take it anymore and had to press the nurse call button.

"It was just a cold! It's not like I was going to die!" She sounded more forceful than normal, and I realized she was pushing back at me for my own angry tone earlier. I had let my emotions take over and effectively belittled her mother. I looked guiltily at the ground.

"I... I'm sorry. I shouldn't have talked to your mother like that," I said. "But I wish you would understand why I'm worried. You can say it's just a cold, that you're fine, but they haven't let you out of the hospital yet. Besides, colds do kill people. It happens. You shouldn't be so apathetic about yourself."

"I'm not going to die." She was a bit confused, a bit embarrassed—but she still basically sounded unconcerned. Was I overreacting? Or was she so used to being sick that she was just numb to these things?

"I didn't really think about it when you were just another

kid in class to me, but I've never met anyone whose health is as delicate as yours, Yuki. Each time I hear you've been hospitalized, I'm afraid you're going to die. It's so scary. So now, to find out that you were getting worse and no one even told me, it just…"

She only repeated that she was fine, as I'd known she would. We were parallel lines running beside each other.

A long moment of silence hung between us. Finally, she broke it. "I've always been glad that you love the stars so much, Tasuku. I was happy whenever you'd come and talk to me back in middle school. People who don't share my interests only ever ask how I'm doing. It's always, 'Feeling better?' But all I can say is that nothing's changed. I know it's not their fault, but I feel bad that I can't give them a real answer."

"Ah… I didn't know."

"Yeah. That's why I wanted to get to know you better, because you talked to me about something that interested you. You know, since I met you, I sleep with the window curtains open at night sometimes. The nurses always close them when they come around, but thanks to you, I think the night sky is more interesting than I did before."

"Oh…" I thought of that May evening when she'd been on the phone, looking for that constellation. I thought of other times, even before that, when I had looked up at the night sky with her.

"And I know your test isn't for some special qualification or whatever, but I see how hard you work on studying for it, even when we're together. I wish you wouldn't act like it wasn't important." She pursed her lips, which only accentuated the lines of her painfully thin cheeks. That was what stopped me from agreeing completely with what she was saying.

"Could you at least tell me, then, if you have a fever or catch a cold? I won't be able to concentrate on studying if I think you might be hiding something from me, and then when I find out, I'll feel like you don't trust me. I know I'm not family, that maybe you can't tell me *everything*, but still…"

She looked straight at me. "Tasuku…"

I didn't want to see the expression on her face. I grabbed my bag and stood up, looking down the whole time. "All right. I guess I'll go home," I said.

Yuki's mom was waiting outside her room. "I'm sorry for what I said to you," I told her with a bow of my head. Then I hurried out of the hospital.

It was the first real fight we'd had since we started dating.

✳✳✳

I was still upset when I got to school the next day. Yuki had sent me a text the night before saying she wanted to talk again, to make sure we understood each other, so I'd agreed to visit her that afternoon. But I was still feeling out of sorts, and it was hard to get excited about it. Our graded exams started coming back to us, but even the fact that I'd gotten a good score wasn't enough to lift my spirits. I knew I'd paid for it by being pushed away from Yuki.

Once our short homeroom meeting was over and I had submitted the daily class reflection, I wanted to head straight home, but it was my day on after-class duty, and I'd been asked to do a few chores. I couldn't leave yet. I even found myself thinking, *I guess that could make a good excuse if I wanted to tell Yuki that I won't be in time for visiting hours.* I sighed to myself.

My partner for after-class duties was Miyano, a guy I hadn't talked to much. He seemed sort of awkward, even as he went to deliver the ethics report he'd gotten from the social studies prep room.

Some people insisted that Miyano's face looked like a girl's, but even when I saw him close-up, I didn't really think so. True, his eyes were on the large side and he seemed particularly thoughtful, but he was just a guy.

I was still lost in thought when a teacher called, "You there—Miyano, right? You're on the Disciplinary Committee, aren't you?"

I watched out of the corner of my eye as Miyano followed the summons to a nearby classroom. As for me, I bowed and showed myself into the hallway. If this was about Disciplinary Committee business, then maybe I could afford to be on my way. Still, I hung around for a few minutes, just to be absolutely sure—and that was when I heard some students prattling on by the stairs.

"A six PM curfew? What are we, middle schoolers? What a prissy little princess. *'Ooh, I have dinner at seven!'* So, what, I rank lower than food?"

"Can you really call her a princess with an appetite like that?"

Someone was busy badmouthing his girlfriend, I guessed.

"Her family is, like...so *normal*! She goes right home on the weekends, too."

I couldn't believe he would insult her like that. Who cared about her schedule? At least he could see her when he wanted to!

"With that curfew, you'd have to split around five PM! God!"

"Don't I know it. This sucks! And to think, she's the one who asked *me* out!"

So walk her home, then!

"You two went to the same middle school, right? Sounds like it could get pretty ugly if you got in a fight."

I stood there listening to the ingrates, getting madder and madder. You could only talk that badly about someone if you didn't care about them, never mind that you were going out. Where did he get off blaming his girlfriend for her curfew? If there'd been a door around, I would have slammed it just to let off some steam.

Without any doors to work off my anger, though, my impulsiveness got the better of me. I stomped into the hallway and glared up at the guys on the landing from the bottom of the stairs. "I'm sick of listening to you! What gives you the right to talk that kind of shit about a person?"

Their eyes locked onto me. Even with the sun at their backs and faces in shadow, I could feel them looking at me with contempt.

"'*Scuse* me?" There was that unmistakable crackle in the air that you only felt when someone was really, really pissed off.

Well, now I've done it.

"Er..." My throat hurt as a sharp breath escaped me.

I made an instinctive decision: *run*. Dashing away, I flung myself through a nearby open window. I'm not a fast runner, so my plan was to find somewhere to hide. Unfortunately, it was only after landing behind the school that I realized I'd made a huge mistake. My bag was still in the classroom. I'd have to go back for it. I'd left Miyano all on his own, too. Crap. The angry guy wouldn't think Miyano was me, but he might take his anger out on him anyway. Maybe it would have been a better plan to race back to the social studies prep room and find help.

Didn't matter now. I had to try to get away. Perhaps I could go around the side of the building and make my way back to the classroom. The exterior fire exit seemed like a good, safe path back to my bag.

I was hurrying along, thinking about the hopelessness of the situation, when I thought I heard Miyano's voice. I was probably imagining things, or maybe my hearing had gotten sharper, like a prey animal being pursued by predators.

I was immensely lucky. My snap decision to jump outside had sent the angry guys running down a nearby hallway, shouting all the while. I breathed a sigh of relief as they went by.

Argh. What am I doing? I thought. I'd just been lashing out. I'd had a fight with my girlfriend, whom I cherished, but the real reason we'd argued was because each of us wished the other would be less concerned about them. The Star Test was just a hobby thing for me. Yuki was more important, but she was trying to keep me from worrying about her because of a condition that was just par for the course as far as she was concerned.

We aren't actually upset with each other, I realized. In fact, the problem was that we were both trying to care for the other the best way we knew how. I hated the feeling that Yuki was holding out on me, but I didn't and wouldn't hate *her* for it. If anything, I loved her more than ever.

I'm so completely smitten...

I remembered the thought of using after-class duty as an excuse to get out of visiting her. But no, I decided I was going to go.

Right at that moment, I heard a very angry shout: "There he is! That's the guy!"

Still crouching, I froze where I was. I wanted to run again, but my body wouldn't move. The next thing I knew, I was being kicked in the stomach, and as I rolled on the ground, someone hit and punched me. I tried to find an opportunity to escape, but I was surrounded, the blows coming one after another.

They're gonna murder me! Did that really happen? My mind went blank with disbelief. Here I was being punched and kicked at my own school, where I went to learn every day. This couldn't be real, could it? I curled up against the pain, my breath coming hard, and willed myself to stand. I had to get away. Fast. I had to get out of here!

My panicking brain was assaulted by another blow, and there was a nasty crack as the frames of my glasses bent.

I'm done for...

In the moment I resigned myself to my fate, though, the beating suddenly stopped.

"Who the hell are you?" one of my attackers demanded.

"Pipe down. I'm trying to clean up here," said an unfamiliar voice. The voice of my rescuer.

"What?! How dare y—oww!"

My assailants were half crouched, but the mysterious newcomer had stepped on one of their feet. It wasn't a kick, just a stomp.

"That *hurt!*" the punk bellowed, enraged to have been interrupted.

No, I thought, suddenly calm, *I'll bet it didn't.*

"Are you in one piece? Better move," the new voice said serenely.

"Y-yeah," I said, and scrambled backward. My skewed glasses left my vision blurry. Whoever it was stood between me and the bad guys, protecting my retreat.

"Hey, you! You better not screw with us!" one of the bullies said.

"Did you hear me? I said I'm trying to clean." He was

sticking to the nice-guy act. From what I could see, he looked like an upperclassman, tall and well-built. He looked like he could hold his own.

I continued scrambling in the direction of the school building when I heard someone whisper, "Over here!" It was Miyano, who had a broom and trash bag by his feet.

I guess the guy really was cleaning.

"Can you walk? We've got to get you to the nurse's office." Miyano held out his hand. I took it and got unsteadily to my feet—and then I ran.

I got some first aid and gave a quick statement in the Disciplinary Committee room—then I broke my promise to go see Yuki. My face was puffed up, I was aching, and I had to do something about my glasses. She would know I'd been in a fight. When she found out I'd picked it myself to blow off some steam, only to end up getting beaten up, she wouldn't be happy. And the way I looked, I knew she would worry about me. After much agonizing, I sent her a text. Sorry. Don't think I can make it for the next two or three days.

I didn't give a reason.

I didn't have any broken bones, but I did get some ugly bruises on my stomach that excused me from swim class. Thankfully, I could get a decent grade on the practical-skills part of the class based on what I'd already done, and I wouldn't be penalized for observing. Honestly, it was a relief; I'd never really liked swimming.

My relief didn't last long, though: I knew I couldn't put off seeing Yuki any more. My glasses had been easy enough to repair—the lenses weren't cracked, so I'd just picked similar frames and had them swapped out. But you could still see the bruises on my face. Well, I was just going to have to bite the bullet.

"Hey," I said, knocking and then slowly sliding open the door to her room.

"Hey, Tasu—ohmygod!"

I was trying to keep my head down as I came in, but I guess it wasn't enough. Shock and concern came over her face. All I could do was nod. "I kinda got hurt."

"It looks like more than *kinda*!" Her big eyes started to well. She must have been really shocked. I'd already seen my family's reaction to my injuries. I knew how upset she would be to see someone she cared about had obviously suffered from violence.

"I'm sorry," I said after a second. "The day I told you I couldn't come, it was because...well, because of this. It's not as bad as it looks." I slid the round stool over to her bedside and sat beside her. No sooner had I sat down than an adorable little punch landed on my shoulder. It didn't hurt at all; in fact, I sort of smiled.

Her voice, though, was sharp. "I don't mind that you couldn't come, but I wish you'd told me why."

"...Yeah," I said. I understood.

"Did you get in a fight? Who with?"

"There was this guy at school. I didn't know him, but he was talking crap about his girlfriend. Shouting it all over the hall. It pissed me off, and I told him to shut up...which earned me a beating."

I threw my head down on her bed, *pompf*. She sighed, then after a moment, she positioned my head on her knees, her hand brushing gently through my hair. "Did you at least get in a hit back?"

"Not even close. I tried to run away, but they caught me, and that's when they really gave it to me."

She sighed and gave me a karate chop—with the same hand that had been so gentle with me just a second before. Here I'd hoped an honest confession might make things easier. Her blow landed on my bruised cheek, and it hurt, but I smiled in spite of myself. I heard another exasperated sigh from above me, but I thought I could catch kindness in it, too.

"Listen, Yuki... About last time. I said some terrible things to your mother," I started. It was a low blow to bring up the death of her beloved daughter. Even if I hadn't *acted* rude, it must have hurt her very much. Yuki's family had been through everything with her. How could it not hurt them to see their daughter constantly in and out of the hospital? I felt pathetic.

"Yes, you did," she said. After a second, she went on, "My parents actually really care about you, Tasuku. They even said you're like a son to them. I think that's maybe, uh, going a *little* far at the moment...but that's why they don't want to interrupt your studying. They see how hard you're working. And I definitely agree with them about that."

"I had no idea..."

"Hee-hee."

I care about them, too.

Until a few days ago, I probably would have argued with her about her parents, but now I could see how wrong I was. We weren't in a competition, her parents and me, and even though I thought their attempt to be considerate had backfired, I no longer blamed them for it. They were trying to do what they thought was best for me.

I realized that my frustration and unhappiness about Yuki's illness had made me weak at heart. I said things I should have kept to myself, lashed out at the people around me. I was profoundly embarrassed by myself.

"I love you," I said.

I might have realized it was wrong to behave the way I had, but that didn't make my anxiety go away. I couldn't go without Yuki. I'd never cared so much about anyone before. Even if I knew that was a lot to put on a person. Still, I couldn't go blaming my inexperience for letting myself get swept up by my emotions...

I slowly raised my head. I didn't want this to be something I only said when we were cuddling—I wanted to be able to look her in the eye and tell her.

"I really do love you."

I saw the blush in her cheeks, bashful and overjoyed at the same time. I loved her smile so much, I could hardly stand it. I loved her quiet laughter. Her slim fingers. Everything.

"I'm gonna get healthy," she said.

"I know," I answered. "I'll be here."

She said it to reassure me, but I knew she meant it, too. I could see the marks from the IV line on her wrist. I clasped her hand, scars and all.

In class, we start out the year seated in Japanese alphabetical order. Since my name starts with *M*, which comes near the end of that sequence, I'm always one of the last to introduce myself. I'm never sure what to do. They tell you to talk about your favorite things or what makes you an interesting person or whatever, but I've never been very good at that.

"I'm Tasuku Kuresawa. I chose this school because it has an Astronomy Club. As a point of interest, I have a girlfriend. I look forward to spending this year with you."

There was an appreciative buzz from the rest of the class. It was the day after the entrance ceremony, and we were all introducing ourselves, which meant talking about a lot of purposefully inoffensive subjects. Playing the girlfriend card earned Kuresawa some serious attention.

Astronomy Club? Do we have one of those? I thought. This Kuresawa guy seemed awfully romantic, and that made him memorable.

My reasons for picking this school weren't as well defined as his. I'd wanted an all-boys place that was easy to commute to from my house and that would offer lots of possibilities for the future. Since I still didn't really know what I wanted to do in the future, keeping my options open seemed like the best course of action.

All I'm really saying is that everyone sitting there in the classroom with me had different reasons for attending this school. As Kuresawa just demonstrated.

It was the first time that I, Yoshikazu Miyano, sat up and took notice of Kuresawa. I ended up joining the Disciplinary Committee and the Literature Club, so I didn't see a whole lot of him. My days were fulfilling in their own way, but as far as Kuresawa went, I figured we'd be classmates all year and nothing else. Until one particular day proved me wrong.

✳✳✳

They're after us!

One afternoon, not long after first-term finals, I found myself being chased. Seriously.

I ducked out from behind the south building, where the trouble had started, looking for anywhere we might be able to hide. Then we darted into the school itself, keeping an eye out.

I say they were after "us," but in actuality, I was trying to help Kuresawa escape the vicious beating he'd been receiving. Even if I had no idea why he'd been attacked. All I knew was that a few minutes ago, he'd been with me on after-class duty, and then suddenly, he'd been in the middle of a group of guys kicking and punching him.

Nurse's office, nurse's office... This way. Calm down. I knew I had to stay cool. Kuresawa was hurt.

I'd never actually seen a person punch someone else, never witnessed how brutal a kick could be. It felt more awful than I could have imagined, worse than seeing it in any movie. It would be enough to throw anyone into a panic. Confronted with violence and no one around to break it up, I was hit with the sickening realization that logic and common sense wouldn't get me anywhere in this situation. I was overwhelmed by my own powerlessness—my own inability to put a stop to it.

I wondered if the guy who'd jumped in to help Kuresawa was okay. I'd just happened to bump into him, but he was a lot more help to Kuresawa than I was. All I'd been able to do was cry for help in sheer shock. Before he'd joined the fray, we'd alerted Hirano, an upperclassman on the Disciplinary Committee, so at least the guy wouldn't be high and dry with no one to help him if he needed it—but it was still scary.

The chaos left my heart racing, pounding so hard that even breathing was somehow painful.

"Excuse me! Nurse?" I called, knocking on the door to the nurse's office when we finally arrived.

To my great relief, a voice said, "Yes? Come in." It was just a few words, but they were spoken gently.

I've got to explain, I thought, but my voice wouldn't come out. The sight of violence on the grounds of my own school, even if I hadn't been directly involved, left me so fearful and shocked that my body froze and I couldn't seem to shake it off. I could feel Kuresawa leaning on my right shoulder. Could I possibly manage to explain that he'd been ganged up on?

My concern only lasted for an instant. The moment the

nurse turned to us, her expression changed. "He's hurt! What in the world happened?!"

"Some guys beat him up!" I said.

"Let's start by getting you some first aid. Can you tell me your name and class?" she asked Kuresawa.

"Yeah..." I thought he might need to lie down in bed, but he only sat in a chair and was able to answer the nurse's questions. It almost made his swollen face and the twisted frame of his glasses look even more painful. Maybe it was the injuries to his abdomen that made him hunch forward. Even though we hadn't talked much, I had a strong memory of Kuresawa sitting with perfect posture as he typed on his cell phone.

"Let me see your stomach," I heard the nurse say, and she rolled up his shirt. I found myself facing Kuresawa's back. The nurse decided Kuresawa didn't have any really serious injuries, but my blood still ran cold at the memory of him lying on the ground, cringing under those blows.

I wonder if that upperclassman's okay...

He was pretty much the picture of a well-built guy—broad shoulders giving him a striking silhouette. He'd been so...cool. The sheer calm in his sharp eyes had taken the edge off my own anxiety, but it had almost killed me to have to run away and leave him there by himself. Not to mention I'd left the broom and trash bag (which didn't belong to me!) leaning against the wall. Even if it was to help Kuresawa escape.

I couldn't stop wondering about the guy and whether he was hurt. Once the thought was in my head, I couldn't get it out again.

I flipped open my phone and found a missed call and text from Hirano. Got to the scene, but the guys ran away. You okay? The time stamp showed it had been a good five minutes since he'd sent the message. I'd better let him know I was all right.

I'm fine, thanks, I wrote back. We're at the nurse's office. I hurriedly hit Send, then suddenly realized I'd forgotten something very important. I sent a follow-up: If that other guy is still with you, tell him thanks for his help.

Hirano's reply came almost immediately. I told him. That guy's a classmate of mine. He's fine. We're talking to the faculty adviser in the Disciplinary Committee room. We'd like to get some details. Could you and the guy who got beat up come here?

The tone of the message was a little less formal than I was used to from Hirano, but it was obvious that he was taking this seriously, and I appreciated that. My real fear had been that he would just pass it off and then the bullies would get back at me. Maybe it came from steeping too long in two-dimensional stuff (okay, BL), but it was a serious problem. With a sigh of relief, I slid my phone back into my pocket.

That was when someone said, "You saved my skin. Thanks." I looked up to find Kuresawa looking right at me.

"I'm still doing first aid, young man! Face this way!" the nurse snapped.

"Yes, ma'am," he said, looking not at all concerned as he turned toward her. Come to think of it, even when he'd been getting beat up, he hadn't put his head down; he'd tried to look his attackers in the eyes the whole time. "Thank you, Miyano," he said again.

"Sure, no problem... Heck, I didn't do anything. It was another guy who jumped in to save you." I was annoyed that it was the most I could offer—I didn't actually know the name of Hirano's friend. Some help I was.

"That's not true. My stomach hurt too bad to walk, and you let me lean on you. Thanks for that. I wonder how that guy's doing. I'll have to be sure to thank him, too."

"An upperclassman on the Disciplinary Committee got in touch with me to let me know he's all right. Unfortunately, the other guys got away."

I hadn't gotten a good look at Kuresawa's assailants, so I didn't know who they might be. That realization suddenly worried me. Kuresawa could probably give eyewitness testimony himself, but would they ever find the guys in a school with so many students? Around here, if you weren't in a club or on a committee together, you might never know who was in the class next door.

"Yeah? Well, anyway, I'm glad he's okay. Where are he and your upperclassman?"

"They went to talk to the teacher in the Disciplinary Committee room. They want to know more about what happened and who attacked you. Would you come with me? They want to hear from you, too."

We waited for the nurse to fill out some paperwork about Kuresawa's treatment, and then Kuresawa got gingerly to his feet. "Yeah, sure."

"How are your injuries?" He'd looked pretty rough while the nurse was treating him, not that I'd been looking too closely or anything.

"Well... I can walk. By the way, you don't have to call me 'you.' Just use my name: Kuresawa."

"Huh? Oh, uh, sure, Kuresawa."

"Thanks again, Miyano."

It only took a few minutes for Hirano and the Disciplinary Committee faculty adviser to ask Kuresawa and me the questions they wanted. They offered to take Kuresawa to the hospital, but he said he would let his parents know and go by himself. They said that was all right—the hospital was walking distance from school—but I couldn't help wondering if he was really going to make it.

In deference to Kuresawa's injuries, they agreed to talk to us another time to get more details. It sounded like there would be other teachers involved, too.

"I'll see you later, then," I said.

"Sure. Careful going home," Hirano replied.

Kuresawa had been evasive about exactly why he'd gotten beat up. Thinking maybe it was a sensitive issue, we agreed I wouldn't be present the next time they talked. No one in the room had wanted to challenge him about his excuse that the other guys had been saying some ugly things and Kuresawa had opened his big mouth. Hirano was even going to talk to the nurse who'd given Kuresawa first aid—he was staying busy. It was good to know we had a dependable upperclassman.

From what I heard during the discussion, actual violence on school grounds was pretty unusual, and it might be more than the Disciplinary Committee could handle on its own. Even if they figured out what to do about it, they still didn't know who had been involved in the fight. Neither Kuresawa nor I had seen the other guy's face, after all. We didn't even know what year he was in. Kuresawa's glasses had been bent during the beating, so he hadn't even been able to see the guy up close.

We were told that Sasaki, the guy who'd jumped in to help, had said that the attacker was probably a first-year. It sounded like Sasaki had been on his way to the nurse's office just as we were leaving—I knew he must have gotten hurt. We'd missed him and hadn't been able to say a proper thank-you.

"Okay, Kuresawa, you wait by the exit. I'll grab your bag," I said. He shook his head, but then put a hand to his neck. Even that simple gesture was obviously painful for him. I didn't want him to overdo it.

"You don't have to. I feel bad putting you to the trouble," he said.

"Not like it's heavy. I'll be fine."

I headed back to the classroom to collect Kuresawa's bag. The handful of students who had still been around earlier were gone now, leaving the classroom nearly empty. It was only an hour later than when I usually left school, but the whole place seemed different.

Even with the visit to the nurse's office and the questioning, barely an hour had passed, which made me realize how quickly the entire brutal incident must have taken place. Hardly as long as it took to clean the classroom after homeroom. It all seemed like a bad dream.

"Thanks, it's a big help. Was there anyone there?" Kuresawa asked as I returned with his bag. He was probably worried about locking up the classroom. That was usually the last thing the guy on after-class duty did before returning the key to the teachers' room. I'd remembered it myself halfway back to him.

I handed Kuresawa his bag and took another look at him. His face really did look painful.

"Yeah, Tashiro was there. I asked him to lock up."

Tashiro was one of our classmates, an upbeat guy who knew how to be the life of the party. If there was a lively discussion taking place in the classroom, you could bet he was in the middle of it. He was quick to laugh and horse around and always seemed to be having fun. He and I didn't exactly have a lot in common, but even someone as different from him as I was found him approachable and easy to talk to.

"I really screwed up," Kuresawa said.

"Tashiro wanted to know what happened. I told him you got beat up."

Tashiro saw me leaving with two bags, one of which belonged to a guy I wasn't that close to. I hadn't taken him for such a perceptive observer. Hirano had asked me not to share too many details since the matter was still under investigation by the Disciplinary Committee, but I gave Tashiro the basics. He was considerate enough that I figured if I mentioned someone getting beat up, he would take the hint and not make too big a deal about it.

Kuresawa managed to put on his shoes, though it looked like bending over was agonizing.

"I see you on your phone a lot during breaks," I remarked.

"Oh, yeah. My girlfriend."

"Right, right. I almost forgot about her."

So that was it. I remembered him mentioning a girlfriend when we'd all introduced ourselves the day after the entrance ceremony. I found my first impression of him, which had stayed in a corner of my mind since that day, overlapping with the way he looked as he stood in front of me now. He'd seemed like the intellectual type; the black-rimmed glasses fit the image exactly. And he had a girlfriend who he was head over heels in love with and texted all the time. Right.

"You look surprised," he said.

"Not surprised. More like I didn't realize you kept in touch with her so much." It was more a kind of "gap moe," the charm of someone turning out to be the opposite of what you expected. Not that I could ever say that out loud.

"Yeah? It's nice to be able to stay connected with the person you love, even if it's not face-to-face."

"Huh…" I knew this wasn't the time, but I found myself grinning—he'd reminded me of the book I'd been reading the day before, and something the pure-hearted *seme* in it had said.

"What are you smirking at, Miyano?"

"Who, me? Nothing! Just thinking how nice it must be to be in love."

"Sure. You're an odd one," he said—but then he laughed. That seemed just like what that seme would have said, too. I'd taken Kuresawa for the serious type, but maybe he was more of a joker than I'd given him credit for.

"You think?"

"What, you want details? Sorry, not in the mood today. Maybe once I get myself together." It sounded like another joke.

I smiled awkwardly. "It's okay. I'm afraid I'd only picture something else."

"Hmm?" Kuresawa raised an eyebrow—he didn't look upset, more like he was trying to put the pieces together. I quickly waved my hands.

"Nothing! It's nothing. Anyway, like the teacher said, make sure you stop by the hospital, okay?"

It was possible for a bone to be fractured even if it didn't hurt that much. The nurse had said Kuresawa probably didn't have any internal injuries, but her office wasn't equipped to check, and the adviser of the Disciplinary Committee agreed that it couldn't hurt to be sure.

"Yeah, I will. Don't like that I'm probably going to have to take off from gym class until this gets better…"

"You like gym?" I asked.

Kuresawa informed me that in fact, he hated it, but his expression was grim. "Since I'm already bad at it, I would hate for an absence to torpedo my grades."

Ah. I nodded. That fit very well with my image of Kuresawa as someone who never wanted to slack off.

"It'll be summer break soon. You might not be able to take the practicals, but if you can shore up your grades with some pen-and-paper tests on health, it might not do too much damage. Maybe I can talk to Coach at lunch tomorrow and see if he'll cut you some slack. It might go better hearing it from a member of the Disciplinary Committee."

We were swimming in gym class. Finals for the term were over, but there were still some practical tests to do. Grades included in-pool swimming, which we hadn't finished yet, but it would be tough for an injured guy like Kuresawa to be part of that. Maybe I could ask for him to be graded based exclusively on the work he'd already completed.

I'd always figured that if you beat up another student, you'd be expelled, but I realized that I'd had a blind spot when it came to supporting the victim of the violence. During the questioning in the Disciplinary Committee room, I'd tried to keep everything at arm's length lest they think I'd been involved in the fighting, but now I saw I wasn't thinking it through. Classes were far more separate in high school than they had been in middle school. If someone didn't tell the gym teacher what had happened, he would probably never know.

"You're a pretty good guy, Miyano. Seriously, I really appreciate the help," Kuresawa said.

"Well, apologies in advance if it turns out I can't help you." I didn't want to get his hopes up just to find out I couldn't do anything for him. He just grinned and said I shouldn't apologize before anything happened.

✳✳✳

"Hey, Miyano, what's the opposite of a seme?"

The question came completely out of the blue one fine afternoon between classes, and it came from Kuresawa. I thought my heart would stop. "Wh-what?! Why would you ask that? Why would you ask *me* that?!"

Had I made some sort of slip? I couldn't think of anything. I looked around, afraid that if I just stood there panicking, I'd eventually say something I'd regret.

"The fact that you have such a strong reaction to that question must mean—"

"Stop! Let's talk about this privately," I said. He was acting like you could just *ask* questions like that! I grabbed Kuresawa's arm and dragged him to a corner of the classroom. It was safer than the hall, which was full of students changing classes.

"This is private?" Kuresawa asked.

"Yeah, close enough. What is it?" I said. I was whispering, but Kuresawa didn't see fit to drop his voice.

"According to my girlfriend, a person who likes BL would say the answer is an *uke*."

"Uh, well, seme means *attack*, so I guess the opposite would obviously be *mamori, defense*."

"I get the feeling you're BS-ing me. I saw you flinch."

I nearly choked. Weren't attack and defense opposites? That's what an ordinary person would think, wasn't it? I had *been* an ordinary person until not long ago, so I was pretty sure I knew. It was scary how quickly that change happened.

Without even realizing it, I'd gone so far that I could never go back to who I was before I'd been awakened to BL.

I mean, I liked it, and that made it enjoyable, but let's put that aside for now.

"So it's true. I can feel it," Kuresawa said, nodding with what seemed to be admiration. But the warning bell was about to sound, and he urged that we should get going.

It had been several days since the incident.

They still hadn't been able to pin down the culprit; in fact, the case was going cold. Other than missing gym class, Kuresawa seemed pretty much normal. He and I started talking a lot, and by now he was one of my better friends in class. Partly that was thanks to proximity—being in the same classroom— but more importantly, we had something in common to talk about: BL.

I was a little surprised Kuresawa had figured out that I liked BL. I hadn't gone out of my way to hide it, but I didn't exactly shout it from the rooftops, either. It turned out his girl-friend liked the stuff too, and after my attempted dodge tipped him off, he pressed me until I fessed up.

"So your girlfriend's a *fujoshi*, huh, Kuresawa?" I said. Kuresawa didn't seem, like, biased or anything—he hadn't teased me about liking BL even though I was a guy, for example—but this was an interest I didn't share with a lot of people around me, and I couldn't help but have some nerves. It put me on edge, but Kuresawa rolled with it.

"I'll let you meet her on one condition: You keep your dirty paws off her," he said evenly. I realized he was playing with me, and it sort of ticked me off. He was obviously the kind who enjoyed observing people's reactions. In other words, he was a perfectly decent guy.

"What are you— Of course I wouldn't touch her! She's someone else's girlfriend!" I said.

"Ha-ha-ha!"

I felt myself relax. At least I didn't have to pretend around Kuresawa. As we bantered back and forth, I even started to feel like we'd been talking together forever. I was so glad it had turned out all right, even when my little hobby had come to light.

I was more worried about the incident of the beating. It was looking like summer break would come without any progress tracking down the perps. I'd all but given up hope—but then things changed.

***

During lunch one day the next week, there was some kind of commotion behind the school, which just happened to be adjacent to the first-year classrooms. I heard angry voices, and then a *smack* of something hitting something else. I hurried to the window, but all I saw was Sasaki standing there by himself. He was bent over, clutching his stomach, obviously in pain.

There wasn't much I could do for him. He wanted to hide this from Hirano (*"If they find out, I'll have to write a self-reflection essay"*), so I couldn't exactly call anyone for help. The most I could do was give him some of the adhesive bandages Kuresawa had with him.

I wondered if this had to do with the notorious incident, although from Sasaki's tone, it sounded like maybe he fought a lot. I wasn't in any position to scold him about it; I just told him to make sure he went to the nurse's office later. He made some awkward jokes about how I was cute and asked if I would go out with him. It made me realize he could be pretty laid-back. But I'm a guy. As if I was going to stumble into a BL cliché like that!

I heard the homeroom teacher telling everyone to take their seats, so I ducked away, Sasaki's jokes still swirling around in my head.

✳✳✳

The day after that, I learned what had really happened. Hirano filled me in when we met in the Disciplinary Committee room.

When Sasaki had come back to the classroom, Hirano had pressed him about his injuries. Eventually, Sasaki admitted that he'd been attacked by a group of guys. It wasn't a committee-meeting day, but Hirano decided to make time to ask more questions after school.

Sasaki's attackers had been the same guys who had cornered Kuresawa. Sasaki hadn't laid a finger on them, just absorbed the hits. Just like he had last time, as it turned out. In other words, they were out for revenge, and he had simply taken it.

As Hirano talked, I felt myself go numb. Why had I assumed it was a fight? I knew that Sasaki was kind enough to intervene to stop an act of violence; I knew that he always came across as a good person. Nothing like a short-tempered brawler. How could I not have realized that Sasaki had gotten hurt without dishing it back out? With the attackers still on the loose, I should have known they would come after the guy who had jumped in to stop them. I wished I had dragged Sasaki to the nurse's office instead of just telling him he should go.

Why had I thought he fought a lot? I was still depressed as the talk moved on.

Hirano, who was both Sasaki's friend and a member of the Disciplinary Committee, was on the warpath trying to find out who had done it. Even the vice chairman of the committee, the normally unflappable Hanzawa, seemed pretty mad. Although some of their frustration appeared to be annoyance at Sasaki himself, who'd misled them by claiming that he'd "been in a fight" instead of simply "been attacked."

"He can't stay out of trouble, that guy" was Hirano's assessment. It sounded like if someone hadn't gone after the perp, Sasaki would simply have let himself be beat to a pulp. The thought pained me.

But why?

***

We spent the entire committee meeting on the incident, naturally. It resulted in us spending lunchtime looking for any witnesses. People tended to eat lunch in the same place each day, so we went around to any groups sitting on benches near where the attack took place and asked anyone who might have been walking by around that time for information. We knew the perpetrators were first-years, and this time Sasaki had gotten a pretty good look at them, so we had a lot of circumstantial evidence.

We also called on Kuresawa again, as a witness to the previous incident. We were going to figure this out. It would help that Kuresawa had a doctor's note attesting to his injuries.

* * *

"Is it true Sasaki got attacked, Miyano?" Kuresawa whispered to me as soon as I got back to the classroom after lunch.

I nodded discreetly. "Yeah. You probably heard already that they want you in the Disciplinary Committee room again after school today."

I hadn't told Kuresawa exactly what had happened to Sasaki at lunch two days before. He only knew he'd been hurt. At the time, I'd said a friend of mine had scraped himself up and asked if Kuresawa had any bandages. I even kept quiet about the fact that Sasaki was sitting just behind the school.

"Yeah, I heard," Kuresawa said. "This is all my fault."

"No, it isn't," I said, thinking of Sasaki. How brave he looked protecting an underclassman. The gallantry he showed by refusing to lay a hand on the bullies even though he was bigger than they were. But also the indifference to his own welfare that could make him a magnet for trouble, just like Hirano said.

I don't understand him, I thought. Just moments after he'd been beaten up, he'd been laughing and joking about whether I would go out with him. He'd practically looked like he was enjoying himself. That was why I'd assumed he wasn't very serious.

"You're being pretty quiet, Miyano."

Shoot. Was it that obvious?

"I was just thinking, I was virtually on the scene. But I didn't realize what had happened until Hirano spelled it out for me today. I can't help thinking that if I'd figured it out sooner, I could have called a teacher, and we might have caught those guys already." The regret almost suffocated me.

"How was our upperclassman doing at that moment?"

"Uh, pretty much fine, I guess. He was laughing."

"Then I'll bet he didn't want you to take it too seriously. Don't let him see the look on your face right now!"

"Maybe. But..."

"But you want to crack this case, right?"

I nodded. He was right. Sinking into a depression wouldn't change anything. Something might even happen to Kuresawa at this rate, and anyway, I didn't want to rely on Sasaki forever. As a member of the Disciplinary Committee, I had to do what I could.

Sasaki, I thought. I could still see him laughing, having fun. I didn't know him very well yet, but I knew one thing: I wished he could always laugh like that.

"Wanna go out with me?"

It would be a while before I discovered his offer was no joke.

Now that I was a second-year, I had underclassmen to think about.

"You *have* to listen to me, Hirano!"

"No, I really don't."

My name is Taiga Hirano, and I found myself the confidant of Miyano, a younger guy on the Disciplinary Committee. From his irrepressible energy at that moment, you would never have guessed that there had been a time when he'd been pretty cheerless.

"And you could stand to tell me at least a little of what happens between you and your roommate!"

"Also no."

This was how it always seemed to go with us. But me, I let my mind wander back to when we'd just met.

✳✳✳

After school one day in early April, not long after classes had started, the Disciplinary Committee had its first meeting. Two people were picked from each class to be members, and the new kids' unmistakable nerves put tension in the air. It felt like my shirt wasn't fitting me right.

The committee members were all introducing themselves to start the year off. "My name is Yoshikazu Miyano," one of the new kids was saying. "I look forward to being on the committee with you this year."

Yoshikazu? Not sure I recognize that name. I glanced down at the list of members, and there he was: Yoshikazu Miyano. First-year. *Look at that.* The characters for his name were appealing; they had meanings like *palace field* and *beautiful*. But the name itself, Yoshikazu Miyano, sounded elaborate and formal.

I kept my eyes on him as he sat down, still looking nervous. He happened to glance in my direction at that exact moment, but our eyes didn't meet—because he was busy looking at my head. He wasn't the only one. Other students had been stealing glances my way during the introductions, too.

This guy smells like an overachiever, I thought. From the way he bowed his head as he greeted us to the way he talked, everything about his behavior and attitude was impeccable. He didn't seem like the type who would see eye to eye with a rough-looking guy like me.

Hanzawa, sitting beside me, saw the stares, too. "Look who's the center of attention," he whispered with a grin. Everyone wanted to know why a member of the Disciplinary Committee had gold hair. It didn't help that they each had a copy of a handout detailing the criteria used when the committee did inspections. All the first-years were curious, but most of them hid it better than Miyano. Hanzawa's grin only got wider as he said, "He looks like the kind who loves his work."

He was right. Miyano turned out to be a very good worker. He was serious about his time at school; his conduct irreproachable. True, he always looked like he wanted to say something about my hair, and that wasn't something I could brush aside by just acting more upperclassman-y. If he was a little intimidated by me, let him be. I figured I would just keep an eye on him from a distance.

Whatever he thought of me, I learned very quickly that Miyano would tackle whatever job he was given. Hanzawa saw it too, and he was excellent at putting him to good use. In fact, Hanzawa was so skilled at helping people who felt out of place to be more comfortable that he was the dorm leader this year. With Hanzawa's encouragement, Miyano learned to stop bailing out of conversations. Gradually, Miyano went from reticent to willing to talk, and it felt like his walls were starting to come down, at least with Hanzawa.

It was right about then that a turning point came in the form of some guys beating up a fellow student on school grounds.

By sheer chance, Miyano had been near the scene, and he came to me for help. I was surprised that he turned to me and not the more-approachable Hanzawa. Maybe my rough appearance made him think I would be better in a fight.

I wasn't able to help immediately; by the time I got there, all I found was an injured Sasaki—and that really surprised me. I asked him about it, but it turned out he wasn't particularly close to either Miyano or the student who'd been getting beaten up. He'd just jumped in to help.

That left me at a bit of a loss. "I thought you said you didn't like fighting, 'cause you're not any good at it," I said, showing him the grateful text message Miyano had sent me.

"Ugh... I must look like a total dork," Sasaki said.

"Oh, please," I replied. What about jumping into a fight to help someone was dorky? Although I didn't say it, I was also grateful to him for helping to keep an underclassman safe. I hadn't thought Sasaki would do something like that. I felt like I was witnessing a moment of dizzying change.

The feeling passed quickly, because ever since the incident, Miyano's behavior had changed visibly. He was a lot more tight-lipped, and each time he saw me, his expression darkened. He would look at me like he wished he could say something, then after a moment's hesitation, swallow the words again.

That wasn't new, as far as things usually went. It was just part of his personality—you could call it seriousness, if you were feeling generous; inflexibility if you weren't. But today, it struck me as something I shouldn't just ignore. Call it an upperclassman's intuition. (Even if I hadn't been an upperclassman for very long.)

It was taking us days to crack the case, and at first I thought Miyano was on edge because it felt like the attackers could be anyone. But even after we figured out who'd done it—just before summer break—he kept acting funny. If anything, he seemed stranger than before.

I conferred with Hanzawa, and we agreed that he was in high school now, and it would be better to just keep an eye on him and see how he was doing rather than trying to force him to talk about some passing mood. It didn't seem to be working for us, though, so shortly after the start of second term, I asked Miyano to talk to me in the Disciplinary Committee room.

✳✳✳

"I get the feeling there's something you'd like to say to me," I said. Miyano had looked all out of sorts from the moment we'd sat down. I thought maybe he was still feeling frazzled from the all-too-short summer break, but I also heard him murmuring about "what's with this situation" or something.

"Uh... Umm..."

"You can tell me. I promise I won't get angry. Really, I mean it." People told me I was downright frightening when I was asking questions one-on-one, so I was trying to be careful, but Miyano still looked like he thought I was going to kill him.

His voice cracked a little as he said, "R-really? I can tell you...?"

"Yeah. Go ahead."

I could see him screwing up his courage. Then he said, "Hirano, I'm, uh, moe for you."

I couldn't quite process that. "Moe?"

"See, uh, I'm into BL... Like, romance manga. You just seem like you jumped right out of the pages of one of my books, and I can't help getting excited when I see you..."

"What?" Romance? What was he talking about? I mean, I'd known he was into manga, but...

"Take that attack behind the school last term. There's stuff like that in my manga all the time. Well, not so much recently, but it used to happen a lot."

"Really," I said. I didn't quite follow, but I decided to nod along.

"I always used to think it was a stock thing in those kinds of stories, something I could enjoy seeing my favorite artists use. Like the fateful meeting with the guy who comes to rescue

the victim or how your heart pounds when two guys are in love and one of them gets in trouble and the other one shows up just in time to rescue him. I realize now that I always enjoyed them because I knew how they would turn out."

"Hmm," I offered. I knew that just because someone liked manga about tough guys and delinquents, it didn't mean they approved of fighting or bad behavior themselves. Miyano, with his extensive knowledge of manga, probably didn't, either. It must have made this a serious inner conflict for him. It seemed best just to let him talk, so I tried not to interrupt.

He went on. "Now I've seen it with my own eyes, though. I watched a classmate get beat up, and when Sasaki tried to help, he only got hurt, too. I see now that it's not actually that easy to feel moe about." I heard him take a breath. There was a look of self-criticism on his face. "Obviously, there's not that much violence around here, but I still can't shake the thought that maybe it's not okay to get so moe about BL. At the same time, I keep seeing things and thinking, *Oh, that's like something out of a BL manga.*"

He was talking quicker. Maybe he was embarrassed.

"I just wanted to say I'm sorry for thinking of you in those kinds of situations, Hirano. When I'd never want them to happen in real life."

Oh... Me?

Hearing my name at the end of this whole explanation brought it all together. That's why he was telling me. That's why he always looked like he wanted to say something to me. I felt light in a way I hadn't before this conversation.

I slumped in my chair, realizing I'd had it all wrong. "So you weren't just intimidated?" I asked. I thought of my roommate and realized I seemed to have a lot of awfully confident underclassmen around me. "I dunno much about BL. But tell me this stuff instead of keeping it inside, okay?"

I couldn't just laugh it off as something he shouldn't be so dire about. Miyano's distress was obviously real to him, and I could see how it upset him to be questioning something he enjoyed so much.

"Huh?"

"It's sort of like rehabilitation, I guess. This BL stuff means a lot to you, and I appreciate you telling me about it. Long as you don't cause real trouble, I won't get upset."

I wasn't going to tell him to quit his hobby or stop dragging the real world into it or anything like that. I was the one who made him come clean even though he had come straight to me for help. I figured it was on me to see it through to the end.

"Sure, of course…! Thank you very much!"

I was never really the babysitting type. It was only just recently that I had started to see underclassmen as sort of sweet and lovable—only since I'd become an upperclassman myself.

I wonder if Kagi's rubbing off on me, I thought. Dealing with my roommate had definitely given me a new perspective on how to relate to people who were younger than I was. The fact that I could bring that understanding into my committee activities was a pretty noticeable change for me.

Once he had resolved to stop worrying about it, I still saw Miyano giving me furtive looks from time to time, but more and more often he shared his "moe talk" with me and started to seem less reserved. He never let go of the relatively polite way he talked to me, but he didn't hold back, either. It made him seem particularly outgoing among the first-years. He was pretty darn energetic, that was for sure.

His imagination never seemed to quit, either. To my surprise, he asked about "things between me and my roommate" with taxing enthusiasm. He repeatedly alleged that it was "too moe to believe; it can't be real!" Sure. Whatever.

So he was pretty forward with me, but I never felt like he was mocking or insulting me, so even though this kept up for months, I never felt the need to stop him. I let it go in one ear and out the other, just like I'd told him I would.

He started speaking up a lot more in Disciplinary Committee meetings too, even though first-years usually found it intimidating to contribute to the committee's plans. That was partly because of the regimented nature of the committee's agenda, but it's also because the committee's initiatives require so much thought. A lot of the stuff we do deals with details that could be seen as curtailing students' autonomy. Changing any customs or rules was a tricky subject, but Miyano tackled it without ever seeming cowed. He made himself more and more integral every day. He was serious and dedicated but had the willpower to turn down anything that didn't seem right to him. The same qualities that came through in his "moe" stuff.

I guess that's better than someone who keeps his mouth shut and never does anything, I thought. I simply promised myself that I would punch him if he ever crossed the line.

Recently, though, he'd been spending more and more time with Sasaki, so I heard fewer of his tales of moe. At first, I guessed it was mostly Sasaki who insisted on talking to Miyano, but before any of us knew it, they were fast friends. I worried that Miyano might pick up Sasaki's magnetism for trouble but only briefly. If anything, it started to seem like Sasaki was less tardy than before, thanks to Miyano.

I'd planned to intervene if Miyano seemed like he was

bothering Sasaki—or vice versa—but it's hard to tell how two guys are getting along from the outside. I decided it wasn't cool to stick my nose in. Instead, I just kept an eye on my classmate. I watched the changes in him; he started exchanging books with this underclassman.

Hey, maybe he'd stumbled on someone who would be a good influence on him.

CHAPTER
4 | LOVE & PASSION.

Gonzaburo Tashiro, first-year. At the moment, I'm facing an insurmountable barrier. Namely, the fact that I can't get out of the Ping-Pong Club. Even though I was *supposedly* only dipping a toe in it.

If I wanted to leave the club, there's only one way: I had to defeat the club president in a game of ping-pong. If I was going to overcome an adversary I couldn't even keep up with when we were doing practice drills, I was going to need a very special plan.

Namely, I was secretly doing rigorous extra practice on the side. That was intended to be my ace in the hole. But while I was busy practicing away, I didn't know that from the moment I'd joined the club (thinking it was temporary!), I'd been tagged as a potential future president myself.

***

I felt the breeze. A second later, there was a *wssh* of wind. Gah! Damn. I totally missed my mark. I was trying to end the volley with a big smash, but instead the ball came back my way. I failed to return it, and it was another point against me.

I resumed my stance, paddle at the ready, aware of how intense that volley had been.

"Knock 'em dead, Tashiro!" my friend shouted, but he didn't sound very convinced.

I didn't even have the wherewithal to turn and look at him as I said, "Believe me, I'm trying!"

On the far side of the table from me was the president of the Ping-Pong Club. I had to win this set if I wanted to have any chance of victory, but right now I wasn't seeing a way to do it. I was reeling. I had no idea people played ping-pong at this level in high school.

How the hell 'm I supposed to beat a third-year anyway?! My friend Shirahama had faced another first-year—but me? I got this! How could they have stacked the deck against me like this?!

I knew complaining would get me nowhere, so I sucked it up and faced the table, but I was breathing hard. The gulf between points loomed, announcing my imminent defeat. And with that defeat, I would be inducted as an official member of the Ping-Pong Club.

Like I said, I'd joined the club casually, figuring I just wouldn't show up if I didn't feel like it, but it turned out things weren't that easy. When I tried to withdraw my provisional membership, I found myself hit with the challenge that I had to defeat a member of the club if I wanted them to accept my withdrawal. It was outrageous. And my alleged friend Kyouji Shirahama was behind it all.

He was the one who'd said, "Hey, you like ping-pong, don't you? How about we sign up? Just to try it." It was his plan to drop in and then duck out again. His opponent had been a first-year, someone else who'd only just joined, and Shirahama had smashed him. But I ended up facing the club president! There was no way I would win.

My naïveté had been my undoing. It's true, I did like ping-pong, and I'd assumed that the Ping-Pong Club wouldn't practice as rigorously as the other athletic teams.

So, so naive. What I discovered when I showed up, assuming it would be easy and fun, was the exact opposite. The club had lots of members, and they were very good at ping-pong. It was obviously going to be hard work. I was out of my depth and decided to back out—which was what left me in my current situation.

With the gauntlet thrown, I felt bad saying, "Naw, I wanna quit, see ya." These people were working hard. I didn't want to just show up, spit on them, and leave again with bad feelings all around. But, to reiterate, it was impossible for me to beat the club president. He was so much better than I was that I thought I might pass out from the sheer skill difference. This wasn't one of those things where the more anxious I got, the more mistakes I made. No, it was a simple matter of one player being impossibly, crushingly better than the other.

How many more times would I hear the squeak of my shoes across the floor? Even as I was considering the question, he took another point off me.

"Game, set!" announced the referee, a second-year.

Man, he sounds so cool saying that.

The president's name was circled on the whiteboard containing the tournament bracket. I wiped my face with one of my rolled-up sleeves, my eyes only half open.

It's over. I lost. I knew I would, but it still stings.

"'Kay, see ya, guys," Shirahama said, and took off, leaving me and my depression behind. We were the only two who had asked to leave the club, but there were still games going on, meant to assess the abilities of the new members.

As I stood there, drooping mentally and physically, I was approached by the guy who had refereed our match—the club's vice president, Hanzawa. He chatted with me and explained what it would mean to be a full member of the club. "We don't ask much of you, but you can't bleach your hair. It shows a lack of good discipline," he said.

"Uh... Seems to me like you're asking plenty," I replied.

"You heard the man, President. What's your call?" Hanzawa called out.

"If he can beat me, he can make his hair whatever color he wants," came the president's answer.

"Urgh..." I groaned loudly.

"You say just what's on your mind, don't you, Tashiro?" Hanzawa said with a smile. It sounded like that was supposed to be a compliment, but I was so despondent about being railroaded into becoming an official club member that it didn't make me feel any better.

There weren't any other clubs I wanted to join, and I really did like ping-pong quite a bit. I just couldn't accept the logical conclusion of those facts. Something inside wouldn't let me.

It's hard to get excited about going to a club you didn't really want to join, and somehow my feet didn't always find their way to practice. And once you skip once or twice, it only gets harder to go on day three. But the Ping-Pong Club only had practice three days a week, so if I skipped the first two, that only left the last one, Friday. The president and vice president would show up at the classroom together to drag me off, and I would end up at the club whether I liked it or not. I was starting to acquire a reputation as a bit of a handful around school, so much so that even some of the second- and third-years would call out when they saw me. What was this, the zoo?!

Once I ended up at the club, I felt compelled to take it seriously, even if I was there under duress. After all, it was fun to see my skills improve.

I felt doubly trapped because nobody even resented me for the fact that I didn't really want to be there. They were all completely accepting of me. Sometimes the other first-years and I would go wherever after class, and I even got to know the upperclassmen. It wasn't like I didn't appreciate having some friends from the club. I go out of my way not to hold grudges, if I may say so myself, and that seemed to win over the club president.

"I thought Tashiro'd be spoiling for a fight, but he isn't. That's what makes him a genius worthy of being in my inner circle. Remember that, Hanzawa, 'cause when I graduate, you're gonna be the next club president."

"Yes, sir."

"And I think that guy might be a good successor to you!"

That guy?

That guy, like, *this* guy? Me?!

It was just another day in second term, and the club president and vice president were chatting, smiles on their faces— but their conversation left me speechless. Here I was wishing I could quit, and they were looking at me as a prospective future president? I'd never even stuck around a single club this long before, and now I felt more cornered than ever.

I'd played volleyball in elementary school and been on the

track-and-field team in middle school. My all-around athleticism made me something of a pinch player on just about any team that needed me. I always joined clubs and teams on the assumption that I would eventually go play for someone else, so the idea that I might end up as club president shook me to my core.

They can't be serious, can they? Our president wasn't the type to joke about club matters, though, and while Hanzawa might look like he laughed everything off, he had a sharp memory. It was only then that I realized I was truly in a bind.

"I didn't hear anything. Perfect," I said to myself.

It was simple: I just wouldn't accept the offer to become president. The Ping-Pong Club held on to its members longer than most; it was customary for third-years to stay and participate in activities even after the official tournaments were over, so the president didn't resign until December each year. In other words, they wouldn't try to pin this on me until at least December of my second year. There was no point in worrying about it in the second term of my first year. I was sure that by the time he had to pick a successor, Hanzawa would have found someone more appropriate. Someone more serious about the club, maybe.

"No club today, Tashiro?"

I froze, pinned in place by eyes that were unwavering and determined. It was the first day we'd had club since the discussion of who would be the next club president.

"Nah," I said. "You going right home today too, Miyano?" He was normally pretty dedicated to the Disciplinary Committee, which had seemed awfully busy lately.

"Uh-huh. I want to stop by this one bookstore. Make sure I get the special bonus material they're offering."

Miyano had a habit of looking you square in the eye when he talked to you. It could be disconcerting. I guess I mean, like, a little startling. He was a really decent guy, though. He always seemed to be thinking about what other people needed and wanted. I didn't usually understand what he meant when he talked about his favorite stuff, but I got the feeling he didn't necessarily want to be understood. He sure never explained much.

"Oh, you mean the follow-up thing by that author we were talking about? I ordered it, too," said Kuresawa. He hadn't really looked like he was listening, but from the way he interjected the occasional on-topic comment, he evidently had a pretty good idea what was going on. He'd mentioned to me one time that his girlfriend and Miyano shared the same interest, and Kuresawa sometimes asked Miyano for advice about it.

"Wanna go together? The volumes aren't numbered, so it can be tough to tell which is which."

"That'd be a big help."

They walked out of the classroom, chatting amiably, and promptly hit the road.

Miyano's hobby was man-on-man romance comics. I sometimes wondered about that (like, even though he's a guy?), and Miyano explained to me that it wasn't just comics, that there was "lots of stuff" in the hobby. I dunno. Manga and novels and anime were all pretty much the same as far as I was concerned. Kuresawa and Miyano really seemed to enjoy talking about it, so sometimes I would throw them a "What's that mean?" I didn't actually care that much, so I tended to lose track of the explanation halfway through. Oh well. They didn't seem to mind that I didn't understand, and neither did I. I didn't have to get it for us to be friends.

Meanwhile, I'd accomplished my objective of getting out of there before the Ping-Pong Club president dragged me off somewhere, so I said my good-byes to them with a light heart.

Incidentally, Shirahama, the source of all my woes, had joined the basketball team in the meantime.

I waved good-bye to the other guys, but I didn't go straight home. Instead, I headed for the public bath. It was a pretty big place. They had these gorgeous rooms dressed up to look like an old-fashioned hot spring, plus there were rooms to rest and relax in. I'd been a regular there since starting high school. It was cheap, boisterous, and fun, and I loved going there on my way home.

"Heeeeey, Tashiro!" I stopped when I heard someone behind me shouting my name. "Another round today?"

It was Mr. Yamada, an older man with a slightly sketchy smile—and a woman, Ms. Toyoda, stood beside him. They were old enough to be my grandparents, but they'd been happy to shoot the breeze with me ever since we first met. It felt different talking to older people rather than guys my own age, and I enjoyed when people took time out for me, so I was always glad to see them.

"Hey! You know it!" I kept a washcloth in my bag. That was all you needed—soap was provided. I told people the washcloth was something I needed at the club. That was half true; it was about fifty-fifty between that and the bath.

Because on the second floor of the public bath was a rec room with a ping-pong table.

I know it's the same thing, but it feels completely different.

When we played at the bath, we took our cue from the major tournaments in defining a match win as the first to win three games. At the moment, I was busy giving up my eleventh point as I failed to return a ball that had an inhuman amount of spin on it. It was enough to make me wonder if we were using the same paddle. Anyway, that was the third game—my loss.

"Aw, yeah!" Mr. Yamada exclaimed.

I had never once beaten him in a game of ping-pong. The second I thought I had some momentum going, he would turn the tables on me. I'd never even threatened him with a match point. His technique was overwhelming: his positioning, the power he put into the ball, the way he always knew how to receive my shots. A quick look at the score was enough to show just how good he was.

Plus, he was an expert at the mental game. The better I was doing at the beginning of a game, the bigger difference he'd make between our scores in the middle, until he left me virtually crushed. He simply walked away with one game after another. It was psychological warfare.

Even though I knew Mr. Yamada was just toying with me, I still couldn't help but get excited at the start of a game, feeling like I was doing all right. After he shattered my illusions, I would become anxious, and I could never get my rhythm back.

"Dammit! I'm still not even as good as some old fart!" I groaned. It was all I could do, seeing as he'd thrashed me yet again. I had this idea that I would just sweat a little before I got in the bath, but this was how it always ended up, with my pulse high and my head low.

Mr. Yamada smirked. "Yeah, I'm an old fart, and this is how I play ping-pong. Ergo, this is how good an old fart is. That gettin' through to you?" Now he was just mocking me!

"Argh! This sucks! I wanna win!" I snatched a sports drink from my bag and downed the remaining contents in one gulp.

"All right, boys, let's go wash the sweat off, shall we?" Ms. Toyoda said. The little gaggle of us headed downstairs to the bath. There was a railing, but each of us had one armful of our bathing stuff, so it wasn't easy for the older folks. I was trying to get out in front of them, but as I went by, Mr. Yamada suddenly tottered on his feet.

Yikes! I reached out and held him up, but my heart was pounding. I let out a small sigh. "You work yourself too hard, old man. I don't wanna see you get hurt." Old age made it harder to walk, and right now he was tired, too. Even an extra beat picking your feet up could leave you prone to a fall, and I didn't want Mr. Yamada to overdo it.

"I won't get hurt," he grumbled. I could understand—he had his pride, and here was some kid fretting about him—but I felt like I had to say something. It really bothered me. "I know you've got great reflexes, Mr. Yamada, but it's real easy to slip around here." I pressed close to him, insisting that he at least let me hold his stuff. We resumed working our way downstairs, taking it even slower than before. Ms. Toyoda and the others behind me were whispering; I thought I heard someone say the word *grandson*.

After we split off into our respective bathing areas—they were separated by gender—Mr. Yamada started giving me one of his lectures, which is to say a detailed analysis of everything I'd done wrong in our match. There were other veteran ping-pong players around, but he was the most interested in teaching, and he was always nice enough to tutor me. Not to mention he was very good at it. These moments when I got to sit there, sweating and getting his take on where I'd messed up and how I could do better, were special to me. There weren't a lot of chances to get one-on-one instruction from the upperclassmen in the Ping-Pong Club, and the faculty adviser was no ping-pong player. Getting a breakdown of my most recent match almost immediately was great. It would have been even better if I could then incorporate Mr. Yamada's advice into my playing, but I didn't think I was going to get to that point for a while.

Mr. Yamada, with his grasp of psychology, knew that sitting there listening to all the ways you'd screwed up could be pretty depressing, and he was also an expert at getting me fired up again, leaving me feeling almost as if he'd actually been complimenting me.

I dipped into the tub, and before long, I was pouring tepid water over my head. I always seemed to overheat quicker than anyone. In fact, I was starting to feel a little light-headed. "Think I'm gonna get out, Mr. Yamada," I said.

"Sure thing. You never last long, do you?" He added the same little parting shot he always did: "Bath at home's even hotter." I ignored him and ducked out of the bathing area. It still felt a little funny to change back into my school uniform in the changing room of a public bath.

The whole ritual didn't take as long as a club meeting, but I was starting to think I was more suited to these shorter bursts, focused exclusively on a game. Sometimes we had to switch off between games if it was crowded, but everyone was happy to play against me, so I never had to wait long for a vacant table—something else I was thankful for.

"I guess I just don't like being forced…" If, after I'd joined as a provisional member, they'd said, "You can go check out the other clubs, but come back here when you're ready to join something," I might have been more flexible about being part of the Ping-Pong Club. The practice was hard, but the guys were pretty decent, and I enjoyed the unique camaraderie that came from being part of a team that was very, very good.

Not to mention that I envied Mr. Yamada and his buddies. When they talked fondly of the time when they used to be active players, I felt like I was catching glimpses of them and their old teammates.

As I emerged from the humid changing room, I felt a nice, cool breeze on my damp skin. I put down my stuff in one of the relaxation rooms—they were equipped with tatami mats to sit on, as well as sofas—and then I convinced the old guys to treat me to some milk. I swigged it down while it was still cold, and then I splayed myself out on the tatami, feeling so good, I thought I might just drop off to sleep. While I was lounging, Ms. Toyoda and the other members of Team Grandma finished their baths too, so the break room was getting pretty lively.

Apparently, the vogue among the older ladies was *anmitsu* red bean paste. "Come here a second," Ms. Toyoda called, and it turned out there was even some for me. The women had been reminiscing about their school days, and as I sat down to eat, the chatter quickly started up again. There was a lot of *S* this and *yuri* that, short words and abbreviations that made the conversation sound like it was in code. I was only half listening, and while I knew they weren't really talking about English letters or names of flowers—yuri means *lily*—I definitely didn't quite follow.

Finally I asked, "What's yuri?"

"You don't know? It's stories of love between girls!"

"Huh. Haven't heard that one before..." I guess Ms. Toyoda and her friends had been into reading that sort of thing many years ago, and now their interest was being rekindled thanks to their grandchildren. "I didn't realize women liked stories about girl-on-girl love, too..."

An image of Miyano drifted through my mind. I'd always thought his hobby was sort of weird, but maybe I just hadn't realized how widespread it was. We so rarely know what other people's passions are.

"Are you into anything, Tashiro?" Ms. Toyoda asked, and I flinched.

"Uh, me? I dunno. I guess I hadn't really thought about it." I racked my brain for anything I might be passionate about, but nothing came to mind.

"You're all about ping-pong, ain'tcha?" Mr. Yamada shouted. I flinched again. When had he gotten here?

"That's just so I can get strong enough to defeat the club president!"

Yeah, if I only practice in my enemy's house, I'll never beat him! Not if he saw all my moves, all my habits and tells, everything, just because I was a lower-ranking club member.

Mr. Yamada didn't seem convinced. "Excuses, excuses!" It ticked me off to have an adult wave away what I'd said, but the fact was, there was nothing I could say to that.

I have to admit, I had an inkling. An idea of why it was so painful to learn from someone I couldn't beat—someone I just kept losing to. Why it was so much fun to play with Mr. Yamada and Ms. Toyoda, but doing the exact same thing with the club president just…wasn't. Where I got the energy to keep up this secret "training."

It's because I want to win. I want to beat him.

More months passed, and despite countless attempts, I never did beat the club president. And then it was December, so he left the club. Yes, that was late by the standards of the athletic teams, but from my perspective, it was all too early. I'd only been a member of the club, casual or not, for eight months. Not even a year.

"So you're never coming back, President?" I said.

"I ain't President anymore."

"Not the point! I haven't beat you yet…" I clenched my fists, a yawning, lonely feeling of loss opening within me.

"Ahh. You mean the thing about getting to quit if you win? The next president'll keep that promise. Don't you worry."

"What?"

I don't get it. What happened to the loneliness?

The new president—in other words, Hanzawa.

"Lookin' forward to it!" Hanzawa grinned at me. He was plenty good—he would have to be, in order to be entrusted with leadership of the club. I knew he would be a formidable opponent.

"Wha…?" So I was being passed off to the next guy?

As I stood there dumbfounded, Hanzawa patted me on the shoulder and said, "Good luck, man." He seemed so…not even worried. Definitely not like someone I could beat at ping-pong.

Soon December was almost over, and of course, I still hadn't toppled the club president. I wanted to quit, but I couldn't win—but that didn't stop the "new order" from taking shape.

Winter break was too short for us to hold any practice, so my participation percentage in the club went up, and I found myself taking part in a tournament. I actually won my first game against a guy from another school. My heart started to race as I tasted victory for the first time.

I loved the joy of winning, of course, but I also wanted to hear my teammates cheering for me again—to feel the

encouragement their shouts gave me. I'd never felt anything like it before, but I quickly decided I could get used to it.

Sadly, I lost my second match, but I discovered—somewhat to my chagrin—that carrying the reputation of your organization on your shoulders during an individual match was a hard rush to get anywhere else. I even enjoyed cheering for Hanzawa as he worked his way up the bracket. *Damn. This could be dangerous*, I thought.

There might not be any getting out now.

Still, when I saw players from other schools practically weeping when they lost, I couldn't help wondering: What made them so different from me? I didn't have the passion within me to cry when I lost.

Maybe that's what real passion looks like. What did I have, then? It was a tough question. I couldn't beat Hanzawa or Mr. Yamada. In fact, there were lots of opponents among the upperclassmen and, heck, the general population that I couldn't beat. I'd gotten to where I could outdo Shirahama and the other guys my age, but there was still a high wall to scale.

Looking back further, I knew that at first, I'd just hated not being able to beat the former club president. Feeling trapped in the club and not being able to win one stinking game, even my normally laid-back self had gotten pissed off. Maybe finding somewhere to practice outside of school was my little way of getting back at everyone. And it definitely made me happy to see my improvement as I played at the community center or the public bath. But something held me back, a sense that "passion" was reserved for something you really, truly loved. Something you couldn't replace, couldn't even dream of giving up.

Ping-pong isn't exactly the hill I would die on. But then again...

"How about another game, Mr. Yamada?" I exclaimed.

I didn't start breathing hard quite as easily now. I could hold my own, at least some of the time, and I lasted longer in games than before while still keeping my hands and feet really moving. I was even able to take Mr. Yamada's advice quicker, and my vision was clearer than before.

It's like that road I see in front of me is starting to become real. I wasn't in love with the game, but I had an actual goal to work toward in ping-pong, rather than just spiteful, negative reasons for playing.

"Too tired. Pass," Mr. Yamada said.

"What?!"

"How about I take you on, then?" said Mr. Kumano, who'd been refereeing for us. He was an established veteran in his own right, someone Mr. Yamada said was "good at reading people."

This bathhouse really was *a world apart* when it came to ping-pong. Okay, so the "aliens" here kept my head spinning in every game, but I'm sure the reason I'd been able to keep my composure at the tournament was thanks to everything I'd experienced here.

I finished my second game and headed home drenched in sweat. On the train platform, I bumped into Shirahama. The winter sky was dark already, the mist from our mouths catching the faint lights and making it look brighter than it was.

"Tashiro? You're only just going home?" he asked. Come to think of it, he was probably heading back from a team workout himself. He'd told me bitterly about how another first-year had gotten to play in a real game while Shirahama sat on the sidelines. It seemed to have lit a fire under him at practice. Basketball is a team sport, and you need a sense of unity, but the knives can still come out when it comes to who gets to be on the main squad.

The way he looked when he talked about it—I could see how much he loved basketball. The shine on his face had been almost blinding. That had been a month ago. Having played in a real tournament myself since then, I thought I could start to understand how he felt.

"Hey, good to see you," I said.

"You seem chipper."

"I stopped at the bathhouse."

"Oh, that place. How're things? You better than the president yet?"

"Screw you!"

"Thought not."

It was only over summer break that I'd even gotten to where I could beat Shirahama. Making up the gulf in skill between us had been no easy feat, to say nothing of finally claiming that upset victory. Afterward, I had been profoundly encouraged by the sense that I'd beaten someone who was a better athlete than me. It sort of went to my head, although I didn't mention that to this guy who'd been my friend since middle school.

We didn't exactly have a heart-to-heart there on the train platform, but we traded jabs and shot the breeze. It felt good to just *be* together.

I may not have that burning love that Miyano and Ms. Toyoda have, I thought. But this was definitely the number one thing for me right now.

After all, my right to quit the Ping-Pong Club was riding on it!

✳✳✳

"Heeey, Tashiro!" Hanzawa chirped. I froze. I was in my classroom. It was the middle of the day. What was he doing here?

"Urk!" I said. Maybe he'd found out I'd skipped the previous day's meeting. Hanzawa was on the Disciplinary Committee as well as in the Ping-Pong Club, and when their schedules clashed, he usually prioritized the committee. But I guess word of my absence reached him before we even got to club this afternoon.

Thought I'd have a little more time...

My understanding was that the previous day's discussion had been about the new officers' schedule for the next year as well as potential candidates for the next club president. That was about as interesting to me as a buzzing mosquito, considering I wanted out of the club anyway. I'd figured it didn't matter if I was there or not. Apparently I'd been wrong. Hanzawa cornered me and spent the entirety of the midday break forcibly filling me in on what had been said at the meeting. I was left dazed and exhausted.

I was going to grab some extra food! I'm so hungry from gym class...

Unfortunately, the warning bell was about to ring. Well, no use worrying about it now.

"Hey, President, I'm challenging you to a game!" I called.

"Happy to accept! If you show up for club, that is!"

This was where and how I wanted to win more than anything else right now. My current number one objective: take down President Hanzawa.

Gonzaburo Tashiro stakes his youth on a game of ping-pong! The drama begins now! I could practically see the words, wreathed in flames, in my mind. Nothing seemed as scary as that.

"Oh, I'll be there!"

"We're gonna talk about who should be the next club president, too."

"Seems a little early."

"They spend a year shadowing the current president, learning the ropes." Hanzawa sounded like he was in good spirits. I didn't have the faintest idea that was because the "next club president" was me.

Instead, I took a deep breath of the piercing December air and laughed. "Sounds like a big job!" Someone else's big job, I figured.

How could I have forgotten? I'd *heard* them talking about it!

I'm never *gonna get out of the Ping-Pong Club at this rate!*

In the summer of my second year of high school, I, Shuumei Sasaki, bumped into one particular first-year: Miyano. Now summer was turning into fall, and he and I kept getting closer.

"Sooo, Miya, what's this BL thing anyway?" I drawled.

"It's what we call those guy-on-guy love stories you're always borrowing from me," he said after a beat. He was so cute, I couldn't stand it.

"Oh, *those*."

"And I thought I told you to keep that to yourself in public!"

I liked to call him Miya. Yeah, it sounded silly, kind of like a girl's nickname. And yeah, this was an all-boys school, so he was a boy too, but whatever! He's just insanely cute. What was I supposed to say to something like that except, "You're freakin' adorable, Miya!" If there was a better way to respond, I hadn't heard it.

Every time I said he was cute, Miyano would get angry or try to get back at me. Believe me, if I thought there were any other word to use, I would have used it. But the way he made my heart dance in my chest—well! Another day, another chance to say…

"You're so cute, Miya!"

✳✳✳

"Hey, is Hirano here?" our homeroom teacher asked, sliding the classroom door open with a rattle. It was only me and my two friends inside. My friends were both on after-class duty, and me, I was just hanging around because I was putting off going home. "Guess not," the teacher said. He spun on his heel and was about to leave when I threw up my hand.

"Hirano is probably at the Disciplinary Committee meeting, sir. You need anything?"

"Oh, right. Nah. I've got some paperwork he asked for. Thought I'd give it to him if he was around."

"I can make sure he gets it, if you like. I bet he'll be done soon."

"You'd go to that kind of trouble?" the teacher asked.

I didn't blame him for being skeptical; I knew I tended to act like everything was a big headache all the time. Well, call this proof that I was mending my ways. And this *was* kind of a headache, but I was willing to do it anyway.

"It's no rush," the teacher said.

"I've got nothing but time, sir. Actually, I need something at the Disciplinary Committee room myself."

"All right, then. Thanks."

With the materials in my hand and my bag slung over my shoulder, I bid farewell to my friends and left the room. My steps were suddenly much lighter than they had been earlier.

*   *   *

The whole reason I offered to take the teacher's envelope to Hirano was so I would have a pretext to show up at the Disciplinary Committee room. I knew Hirano would get annoyed if an underclassman were to drop in for no reason—but by the same token, as long as you had even the flimsiest excuse, then there was no problem, right? That's what I hoped anyway.

I knew that if Miya had any serious trouble, Hirano would help out—he was the protective type that way. But he didn't try to get between us much these days. It was probably obvious even to an outside observer that Miya and I were bonding.

At least, I thought so.

Hey, it felt good, though. I opened the door to the committee room, thrusting the envelope at Hirano with a friendly "Speedy delivery, from Teach to you!" and a grin at Miya. My timing was perfect—they were just getting ready to leave. "Let's head home together, Miyaaa," I suggested.

"I'll pass. I need to go to the bookstore."

Hirano, clearing some space on the desk, thanked me, and said, "You two go home together?"

"We just happen to live in the same direction," I said.

"Huh." He didn't sound very interested. He was busy pulling some printouts from the envelope.

Doesn't look like he's going to try to stop us, I thought. But while I was busy feeling out Hirano, Miya just about leaped to his feet. "Okay, I'll see you guys later!" he said.

"Sure, see ya," Hirano replied.

"No, Miyaaa, wait!" I cried.

I was about to zip after him, but in a hard voice, he said, "I'm g-going to the bookstore by myself today. I've made up my mind, and you can't change it!" Was that guilt I heard, though?

His fundamental niceness probably made him feel bad pushing me away.

He took off at a quick trot, but—as befitted a member of the Disciplinary Committee and all-around Top Student—he resisted running in the hallway. My legs were a lot longer than his, and I caught up easily in just a few strides. Somehow, even that seemed cute to me.

"You buyin' some BL?" I asked. It seemed likely, given his insistence on going by himself. And if that wasn't the reason, then I was definitely curious what was.

"Y-you can't just *ask* like that!"

Yeah, okay. I still didn't know what had Miya so worked up.

"Wouldn't it be cheaper if we pooled our money?"

"Two guys browsing the BL shelf together?! Every girl in the store would be fantasizing about us!"

"Oh. So that's the problem."

"Yes. It is," he said, and then he turned away as if to emphasize that *alone* meant *alone*. I was afraid that if I pushed too hard, he would just get upset. If the shelf was the problem, though, I thought I had a solution.

"I can just wait by a different shelf," I said.

Miya swallowed whatever objection he'd been about to make. The way his eyes wandered away from me, at once embarrassed and cornered, was extremely compelling. He normally looked right at you when he talked, so this sent a thrill through me.

When we'd first met, he always looked at me sort of guardedly, something he did a lot less since we started talking about his favorite thing. Now there was just a sense that he was trying to judge how much was safe to share. It was cute.

We still weren't super close, though. It was great to learn

more about him and his interests and all, but when it came to things outside his "hobby," I still felt a wall there. I guess some distance was natural between an upperclassman and an underclassman.

But still, I wanna know!

I was a lot more excited to come to school since meeting Miya. Maybe I would have experienced that sooner if I'd joined a club or a committee or something—but I got the sense that what I was feeling about Miya was something different. I'd never had anyone to really *talk* to much, and maybe that explained why I couldn't seem to put this feeling into words. If anything, I sort of wanted to ask Miya if he knew what it was—even though I was feeling it about him! I wondered if he had a name for this connection that my fuzzy, ill-defined thoughts and feelings seemed to be heading toward.

"You're seriously coming? I'm telling you, it's not gonna be that interesting."

"But I want to get to know you better, Miyaaa."

"Why do you always have to be so direct?"

"Hmm? You say something?"

"Nothing..."

We'd already had the same conversation, or slight variations on it, several times by the time I stepped off the train with him. "If you *really* don't want me here, I'll leave," I said.

"I mean, I don't *really* not... I mean, not *really*, really..."

Miya wasn't his most articulate at that moment. I decided to take his stumbling response to mean that he felt a little funny about this but nothing more. All right, then. I would forge ahead.

The place he wanted to go was a big bookstore on the same

train line as our school. Me, I loved little trips like this, getting off at stations you normally just commute straight through, walking the unfamiliar streets, seeing places you'd never really *seen* before. Time itself seemed to flow differently.

"'Kay. I'll be right here," I said, stopping by a rack of fashion magazines. Miya looked relieved. His boyish face, dominated by his eyes, had a way of making him particularly cute when the tension left him.

I'd heard he was born just before the school year started, so he was still fifteen—meaning that calendar-wise, there was a two-year gap between us at the moment. No wonder he looked so cute to me. I didn't think I remembered ever looking so innocent in my entire life.

"You sure about this? It's gonna take me a while."

Gosh, he was so thoughtful. It wasn't like we were on a date or anything; I'd just followed him. He was looking at me with an expression of genuine pity.

"Hmm? Aw, it's fine," I said. "Take your time. I love just hanging out."

"Hanging out," Miya repeated with a hint of a smile. "All right, then. I'll shout when I'm done."

I could tell his mind was already somewhere else. The cuteness was enough to bring a smile to my face. "Sure thing. If we miss each other, we can meet by the exit." I pointed to the bookstore's front door, which faced the train station.

Miya nodded and adjusted his bag on his shoulder. "Sounds good. See you in a bit."

I flipped through the fashion magazines, but nothing caught my interest—maybe it had something to do with the release date. I loosened up with a couple shoulder circles and stepped away from the shelf. I like clothes, but since I usually wore hand-me-downs from my sister's boyfriend, I wasn't exactly on the cutting edge of fashion.

"No Miya yet..." I checked the time on my phone and discovered it hadn't even been five minutes. It looked like I was going to have plenty of time to kill before Miya came to collect me. I was bored. Sure did wish I was with him. He'd said something about not wanting to be together because we'd attract attention, but I wondered if it could really be that bad. Maybe the only way to find out was to go and see.

Where is he, though? Where do they put the, uh, BL? Hmm... Maybe with the manga, I guess?

I was surprised to realize I'd never seen it before. I worked my way through the store, glancing at the labels on each shelf, slowly looking left, then right. *Shounen manga, shoujo manga...*

The books Miya lent me always had the prettiest pictures, so I figured they had to be around here somewhere. *Oh, I saw the TV-series version of this. So it started as a shoujo manga? Funny how many of these titles I recognize, actually...*

I was getting distracted at every turn, but I kept working my way farther from the door until I found the BL corner. No sooner had I approached than I could feel the female customers nearby stealing little glances at me. It was definitely more than just my imagination, and although I wasn't sure why, it didn't make me feel very comfortable.

I couldn't help noticing it was almost *all* female shoppers over here. *I guess it really is unusual for a guy to read BL. Maybe it's as if he were reading shoujo manga.* The shelves were right next to each other—it seemed like a logical conclusion. Just as I was figuring that out, I spotted a familiar face. "Oh! Miyaaa!" I said.

He looked up from the book whose back cover he'd been reading studiously. "Huh? Sasaki?!" A little loud for the inside of a bookstore. That only attracted more looks.

"Whatcha lookin' at?" I asked.

"Er! Uh..."

I sidled over to him and looked at the book he was holding. It had a clever, eye-catching cover design that made it look almost like a style magazine. The only real difference was this thing used drawings instead of photographs. Huh. I had to admit, you didn't see anything quite like that in shounen manga.

"Huh, that's cool!" I said.

I started to let my eyes wander over the spines on the shelf—and then I froze. "Uh..." Most of the books had titles that referred so frankly to sex that I was almost embarrassed to read them. Trying to find something else to do with my eyes, I looked at Miya, but he averted his gaze. He looked like he'd been caught red-handed at...something.

"I'm kinda surprised. I know it's mostly girls who read BL, but the titles sound just like the pornos guys like," I said.

"Yeah, they're from...a pretty intense label," he replied. He looked like he might burst into tears, and for some reason he seemed to be trying to hide the book he was holding in his hand. Even though the title sounded downright tame compared to these others!

"Label?" I asked.

He didn't even pretend to try to look at me as he said, "It's like, uh, the kind of magazine they're in."

"Ahh!" I nodded. That made sense.

Miya got ahold of himself and said, "Wh-what are you doing here anyway?" The whiff of embarrassment that still hung in the air told me he wasn't used to shopping for these books with a friend. He always came on his own and read them by himself.

"Just wondered where you were at. Farthest corner of the store, I see."

I had to admit, the looks from the women around us were starting to get to me. They weren't piercing so much as...curious. I'd never felt this way in a bookstore before. At least not when I was looking at magazines. Did a guy—did Miya—really stand out that much when he was just looking for his favorite books?

Hmmm... I didn't sense any hostility from the women, but they were definitely looking too much. I wished they could act just a little more natural. What a pain.

Then I thought: *It's not good to see everything as a pain. I promised myself I'd stop doing that!*

While I was busy chiding myself, Miya had picked up another book off a pile. A sign next to it boasted that it included a "special bonus content!" Maybe he didn't care about the looks, or maybe he was used to them.

Gotta just enjoy what you enjoy, I guess. Maybe I was making him too conspicuous by standing there. So this was what he'd been warning me about. He really wasn't imagining it!

As if on cue, I heard someone whisper, "Are they a couple?"

I dunno... I thought maybe I could enjoy that little misunderstanding. Miya didn't look like he'd heard. He was too busy picking out books. If it looked like he was getting upset again, I'd just step away. He was furiously flipping things over, looking at covers, totally unaware that I was keeping a protective eye on him. *He's really serious about this.* The sight of him focused on his books, fretting over them, was a little bit like

seeing him dressed in an unfamiliar outfit. I just stood next to him and waited.

I guess we do look a bit like a couple this way. I fought the urge to put a hand on his shoulder and ask what he was so torn over. In fact, I took a step back. If I made him too self-conscious, he might start avoiding me at school. The last thing I wanted was for him to start giving me the slip. He would open up to me as we grew closer. The thought was pleasant in its own way.

"Hey, Miyaaa, you've got time today, right?" I asked.

"Huh? Uh, yeah, I guess…" He gave me a curious look.

"Wanna grab a bite to eat after this? I'm starving!" A fast-food joint, a café—anything would be fine. We were already out and about, so why not hit up one more place?

"Sure, sounds good. I'll just go check out." He was actually smiling at me, a full-face grin! I felt my heart skip a beat seeing how happy he got just being near his favorite things. I couldn't fight the flood of affection. Every day, more things about him seemed so cute to me. What word could I use if not *cute*? I wondered, watching him go. I spotted the word *love* in the title of one of the books he'd grabbed.

Love, huh?

Yeah, that felt right.

I ambled toward the exit, watching Miya make his way over from the register with an expression of pure, unguarded happiness. Even the way he walked along looked cute. I felt a smile spread over my face.

Love was all well and good, but maybe I'd keep thinking of my little underclassman as "cute" for a bit longer.

"Grab that for me, would you, Kagi?"

"Sure thing. Here you go."

My name is Kagiura—Akira Kagiura—which is why my golden-haired roommate, Hirano, calls me Kagi. Hearing that sweet little nickname come out of his mouth still makes my heart beat faster. The dorm leader, Hanzawa, swears he's never heard Hirano give anyone else a nickname.

Personally speaking, no one's ever called me that before. They call me Kagiura, Akira, or Akki. Once, my friends even started calling me by the name of the hero's sword in a video game we were into. But *Kagi*, that was special.

I'd come to high school to play basketball. I never dreamed I would fall in love here. Who had I fallen in love with? Hirano, of course. Okay, so occasionally he defied expectations, but he had a deep compassion and was always decent to me, and life with him was genuinely fulfilling.

Then came November 11, a day when lovers were supposed

to enjoy a special game together. I'd known about it, but I was hazy on the details. So I was surprised when a box of Pocky suddenly appeared before me.

✳✳✳

"Here, Kagiura," Niibashi said.

"What's this?" I asked.

"It's Pocky."

"Well, yeah. I can see that."

I had just been getting up to go to basketball practice when Niibashi stopped me, so I set my bag down on the desk. Niibashi had his pointer fingers stuck straight up by his ears to make an eleven, making him look even more feminine than usual. I guess at least he was polite enough not to stick his fingers right in my face. He had that much going for him.

"Did you know November eleventh is Pocky and Pretz Day? 'Cause it's eleven-eleven, and the snacks sort of look like ones."

I've heard that... I think. I nodded. Guess every day is some sort of celebration somewhere in the world. "Huh," I said.

Niibashi looked annoyed. "Do you know the Pocky Game?" he asked. I suppose he realized that over the six months we'd known each other, he'd always been the comic relief in our conversations and that I didn't really see where he was going with this.

"Er, yeah. You mean, like, where two people each start eating a Pocky stick from opposite ends? I mean, like, people in a relationship..."

"I have here some Pocky I received from a real live human being." He thrust a red snack box in my face. It was just normal Pocky.

"Who?"

"A friend from my club. He said we should play the Pocky Game, but I said no way. I thought it was kind of gross."

"Huh," I said again. Tough life.

I was used to Niibashi's little bouts of pride (he claimed he got the Pocky because he was "cute"), but I could understand where he might see it as loaded. An invitation like that from a regular friend, not a romantic interest, would make anyone think twice.

"Anyway, forget about that," Niibashi said. "I'm giving this to you."

"What? I mean, I'm happy to eat it, but...why?" I took the box from him and stared at it, confused. Maybe it still gave him the heebie-jeebies, and that was why he didn't want it.

Niibashi sighed and looked annoyed again. "I was thinking you could share it with Hirano back at the dorm."

"Uh, sure. Thanks," I said as I picked up my bag. I was curious what Niibashi had in mind, but I'd have to think about it later—there wasn't much time left before practice. I said goodbye and headed for the locker room. I had changed into my practice uniform when I overheard some of the upperclassmen talking. They'd been playing the Pocky Game and had gotten a little too crazy, leading to one of the teachers confiscating their snacks.

Oh... Niibashi said I should share the Pocky with Hirano. Maybe he meant we should play the Pocky Game?

I wasn't sure about that. I had a feeling that if I suggested playing the Pocky Game, Hirano would give me a befuddled "Huh?" Or if I was really lucky, maybe he would just say, "No way."

Yeah, doesn't seem like his kind of thing. But enough

fantasies. Once I got to the gym, there was no time to think about anything else. I pulled on my basketball shoes and hustled to join the team.

The November days were short, the early twilight making them seem even chillier than they actually were. My breath didn't fog as I walked along, but working up a sweat made the cold more acute. I picked up my pace, hurrying down the road from the station. I was almost to the dorm.

Passing by a convenience store, I thought of the Pocky again. It wasn't that I didn't want to do "couple-ish" things with Hirano, but I didn't want to do them if he didn't want to as well. If we weren't both having fun, how was I supposed to enjoy myself?

What about my family? I wondered. My mom and dad seemed like they would play the Pocky Game, laughing at it all the while. I knew they'd always had a lot of fun together, so just the thought warmed my heart. I could practically see my parents, intrigued by this game they'd probably never heard of, and I couldn't help smiling. Why did the idea give me the warm fuzzies? Maybe I was feeling a little homesick.

It's so great to be able to horse around with someone you care about, I thought, hoping I might be able to be like that with Hirano someday. Thinking about it made the walk through the deepening night pleasant. I refused to be depressed if we never made it there. I could all too easily imagine myself getting scared off. Besides, Hirano and I didn't exactly feel like "family" yet.

"Huh?" I had just reached the residential area when I saw a familiar figure ahead and broke into a jog. The golden hair. The uniform. The way they walked... "Hirano!" I called.

He turned as I caught up. "Oh, Kagi," he said, his expression softening.

"Long day, Hirano? Did you have another committee meeting?"

"Yeah. No longer than your day, though. You look like you're in a good mood. What's up?"

"Oh, uh, do I?"

Hirano, for his part, looked wiped. It was unusual for the Disciplinary Committee to go so late. There must have been a lot of work to do. I'd been surprised, when I got to high school, to discover that the committee was run as a club. Our school thought of it as another way for students to practice having autonomy. By their second year, the members of the Disciplinary Committee were ready to handle the real work, so a lot of jobs fell to them. It was more than you could handle if you were trying to play on a sports team at the same time—which made Hanzawa, who not only was the vice chairman of the Disciplinary Committee but also was in the Ping-Pong Club and even our dorm leader, seem superhuman.

"You're grinning," Hirano observed.

"Uh-huh. Guess what. A friend gave me some Pocky today."

"Nice."

"Wanna try the Pocky Game?"

"Huh? No way."

Nailed it.

He clearly wasn't interested. I hadn't expected anything else, but it still sent a stab of disappointment through me. When had I started to mistake a willingness to play the Pocky Game for a real measure of intimacy?

"Didn't think so!" I said.

"What's gotten into you, Kagi?" Hirano gave me a concerned

look. I guess I really did seem a little wild tonight. Behind his intimidating speech, Hirano was sensitive and protective. He was obviously trying to figure out if there was anything going on with me that he could help with.

It wasn't that big a deal. I gave him the short version: "A friend gave it to me as a joke and said I should try the game. Actually, I'm pretty surprised you know about it, Hirano." I tried to act nonchalant.

He responded in kind with a half nod. "Oh, I know about it, all right. I learned about it 'cause half the class seemed to be going loony about it today. It's like a game of chicken with a Pocky stick..." It was obvious from his tone that things had gotten a little out of hand. I could easily imagine a classroom full of guys yukking it up over the Pocky Game.

"Sounds like things got pretty rowdy for you. I wonder if my class will change at all when we're in our second year," I said. It felt like we had started to come together as a class when we did our thing for the cultural fest, but I didn't think we got as worked up about anything as Hirano's class did about that Pocky. I was in the regular class, not the advanced course, and a lot of us were involved in sports or the arts or something. Plenty of people with special talents. By the same token, though, it tended to mean we all wanted different things, and we lacked something unifying. There was only one room for the regular class, so we could expect to spend all three years of high school together.

"I don't think you have to try to change that," Hirano said. As much trouble as it could be for him sometimes, he seemed to like the class he was in.

"Huh," I said mildly as we got to our room. I was just catching glimpses of Hirano's affection, which could be hard to grasp. I desperately wanted a better look. But I felt childish wanting that. I definitely wasn't going to say it out loud.

"Man, I've got so much homework," I groaned. Hirano had headed straight to his desk when we got in the room, and, following his lead, I'd spread my worksheets out on my own desk. If I got started on my homework now, there would be time to ask Hirano for help if I had any trouble. I felt pathetic feeling like I was cornered by the stuff we'd done in class that same day, but the fact was I was getting left behind in several subjects. Rather than pretend it wasn't happening, Hirano had strongly suggested I face it head-on and ask for help with anything I couldn't do myself.

Wait... Why isn't this making any sense? These were supposed to be review sheets. You'd think I could do a little better. I'd tried my hardest, but I was left with a number of blank spaces that made me want to tear out my hair.

I remembered what Hirano had told me: *"Don't expect to learn it all the first time you ask about it. It's totally normal to need to go over it more than once."* The point was not to give up, to not let myself be pulled along by the seductive but ultimately futile path of slacking off. Even if I did find myself at my desk a lot more than I had in middle school.

Basics. These are basics? I looked from my notebook to the worksheets and back, grinding my teeth with the frustration of floundering like this. I searched through my notes for the parts about the problems I couldn't answer. I even opened the textbook and reread the appropriate sections. Then, not exactly full of confidence, I filled in what I could.

Hey, I think I might be able to handle what we did today. We'd just started a new unit, so the problems mostly looked like what we'd done in class. Slowly, they started to make sense to me. Yes, they were basic, but as I worked on them, I found a new way of looking at them. Once I understood what was going on, I could apply that theory, at least a bit.

Hirano was the whole reason I was able to get into this task that demanded so much time and dedication. The pleasure of studying, you might call it. I'd already been stumbling in some subjects even in middle school, but he took to teaching me with a passion. I wanted to rise to the kindness he'd shown me. Even if I still wasn't the best at studying and didn't see myself falling in love with it.

"There!" I finished the homework—*just about flawless*, I thought. I opened the box of Pocky. Hirano was still at his desk, so I decided to relax but quietly.

Y'know, it's been a while since I've had Pocky, I thought, chewing contemplatively. Junk food like this was never enough to quiet my rumbling stomach after basketball practice, so when I bought myself a snack, it was usually a rice ball or something closer to a light meal. I also drank sports drinks and protein shakes, and mostly I tried to avoid candy—but there were times when I couldn't overcome the temptation.

"Hey, it's almost dinnertime," Hirano said. He had turned to me, alerted by the *crack* of the Pocky stick.

"I'm just takin' a break. Got tired from using my brain. Don't worry, I'll eat everything at dinner."

"Including the peppers?"

He had me there. That one hurt. Hirano had saved me from green peppers more than once already.

"Hirano, you're so mean…"

I knew objectively that you weren't supposed to be picky when it came to food, but my repulsion for green peppers was like an involuntary reflex. They practically paralyzed me. Yeah, I know, it was childish.

"Hah!" Hirano laughed and stood, coming over to me. I was still chewing, *nom nom*. I had a front-row seat as Hirano smiled mischievously—proof that he was in a good mood. I gave him a questioning grunt. My mouth was too full of Pocky to ask what he was thinking.

Instead of saying anything, he grabbed the Pocky sticking out of my mouth and pinched a piece off. In the process, the tip of his pointer finger touched my upper lip. My eyes went wide and I made a sound somewhere between *Um, Er,* and *Ah*. I almost couldn't believe my eyes as Hirano popped the piece of Pocky into his mouth.

"Now we're partners in crime. I'm gonna need your help if I can't finish my dinner," he said, smirking at me as I sat there frozen. Then he made to leave the room like nothing had happened.

"Wha? Hirano… Wha?!"

"Bathroom break," he said.

Not what I was asking! My head was swimming with the sensation of his fingertip brushing my lip and the image of him tossing that last bit of Pocky into his mouth. I all but collapsed onto my bed. "Not fair, not fair, not fair, not fair, not fair at all!" I fumed. What he'd done seemed way beyond even the Pocky Game.

I wasn't just imagining it, was I? Part of what had me worked up was that Hirano didn't seem to *mean* anything by it!

Still…if anyone's going to get me riled up, I hope it'll always be him.

I felt my heart pounding from happiness. It almost seemed like a waste to keep this feeling to myself. When Hirano got

back, I would tell him thank you. He'd played the Pocky Game with me, in his own way and at his own distance. It had startled me, sure, but it was great. Maybe I should tell him I wanted to do it again. Although I had a feeling he'd only yell at me for eating too much Pocky.

Homework sucks! I want that wild and crazy student life!

I'd joined a club I'd never expected to, got betrayed by my friend (at least the one time), but overall was having a great time. This is my story—the story of Gonzaburo Tashiro's chaotic and absolutely once-in-a-lifetime school life!

Yeah, okay, enough joking.

Recently, I'd started to take notice of a couple of my classmates. I mean, I've started to worry about them. One of them was Kuresawa, who'd been in some kind of fight first term. The other was Miyano, who seemed to be getting closer and closer to one of our scariest-looking upperclassmen.

We'd been classmates for about six months at this point, and although we shared plenty of friendly chatter, they never did tell me what really happened in those days before summer break. I was starting to think the same upperclassman who was sniffing around Miyano had somehow been involved.

＊＊＊

Today we only had morning classes because there was an event to prepare for. We'd had a short homeroom meeting, and then the day was over, and now I was chatting with Shirahama, who'd been my buddy since middle school.

"You don't have any plans today, right?" I asked. Shirahama was on the basketball team, and their practice schedule was pretty set in stone, so I knew when he was going to be free. Sometimes things changed before a game, though, so I had to make sure.

"Yeah, nothing."

"In that case, I've got an idea. How about we go eat some cake?"

"Cake?" Shirahama looked at me curiously.

"You know how people put up their Christmas decorations once we hit December? Like, all the light displays and everything? Well, I saw the Christmas cakes, and boy, do I want to eat one."

"Hah! Yeah, I feel you."

The displays took over almost immediately after Halloween. They were everywhere, they were inescapable, and they were practically calculated to set a high school guy's stomach growling.

"Let's give ourselves an early Christmas present!"

"Very early. Christmas is still a month away!"

True enough. We had lots of time. But a guy could dream, couldn't he?

"Eh, it's all good. I'm gonna save my *real* Christmas cake feast to have with my girlfriend anyway!"

"You, Tashiro? A girlfriend? Not likely!" Shirahama guffawed. Wow, real nice.

"Hey, you never know!" I shot back. "There could be a love letter waiting for me in my shoe cubby right this minute!"

"Well, if there is, just remember that this is an *all-boys* school."

Gah! He was right! I'd been so blind.

Shirahama could laugh about love letters all he wanted, but I knew he was in the same boat. After all, he didn't have a girlfriend, either.

"Anyway, cake, sure," he said. "How about we get a few other guys? The more, the merrier."

No argument from me. "Sure, I'll go ask them," I said. I immediately got up and went over to where Miyano and Kuresawa were having their usual is-it-a-conversation, is-it-not-a-conversation chat. "Hey, we're gonna grab some cake after this. You guys in?" I said.

They both looked up and answered in unison, "No thanks."

I was kind of impressed by their near harmony. Still, I said, "You never want to go anywhere. What're you so busy with?"

"I've got dinner with my girlfriend tonight."

"Not really asking you, Kuresawa. Coulda guessed your reason."

Everyone in class knew about Kuresawa's girlfriend-first policy. He hadn't talked too much about his personal life during first term, but somehow that was one thing that got around in a hurry.

"I don't really like cake," Miyano said.

I made a sound of surprise. Miyano seemed like such a dessert kind of guy. "You definitely look like the cake-liking type," I said.

"And what look is that, pray tell?" said Miyano, clearly annoyed.

"The cute look." The sullen attitude made him seem even younger than he was.

"Sheer bias! How can you live with yourself, Tashiro?" He glared at me, but it wasn't very intimidating.

Kuresawa, looking exasperated, intervened. "You've been at an all-boys school too long, Tashiro. You're numb."

"I'm not numb to anything! At the entrance ceremony, I thought Miyano was a girl."

"How can you say that?! He's obviously a guy! You want cute, you should see my girlfriend!"

"I'm so glad you're my friend, Kuresawa," Miyano said. Kuresawa nodded, but he wasn't looking at Miyano. He was checking out his phone. It always ended up back at the girlfriend thing with him.

"You could stand to act more like it," he said. I knew he was looking at pictures of his girlfriend—again—but I decided not to say anything. I'd just end up bombarded with lovestruck babble.

"You're both a little…funny," I said instead.

"Yeah?" Kuresawa said.

"You think?" Miyano asked.

No harmonies this time. So close!

"Pretty sure," I replied. I didn't want to break up whatever they had going on here, so I excused myself and went to ask some of our other classmates.

Kuresawa and Miyano were obviously becoming good friends. I hadn't seen them together much in first term, and even now it wasn't like they were with each other all the time. To my surprise, they didn't usually eat lunch together, for example. Instead, Kuresawa prioritized being with his club, and Miyano hung around the Disciplinary Committee. I also discovered that unlike me and Shirahama, Kuresawa and Miyano hadn't gone to the same middle school.

Wonder what their story is, I thought.

On reflection, I realized the first time I'd heard Miyano mention Kuresawa had been before summer break. Kuresawa had been hurt when some other guys attacked him. Miyano and Kuresawa, along with the other members of the Disciplinary Committee and even the committee's faculty adviser, had been conducting searches and questioning people all over school. Didn't seem like the best time for a total bystander to go sticking his nose in.

Whatever happened, some guy named Sasaki seemed to be involved. But it wasn't until October that I figured out even that much. It was then, right about when we switched to our winter uniforms, that Sasaki started popping into our classroom from time to time. He was always looking for Miyano. Usually, they would chat for a while, and then he would leave again. They seemed pretty close—close enough that Miyano, who normally wasn't very forceful, could be heard talking to Sasaki like he really meant it or trading barbs with him.

Sasaki seemed like Miyano's polar opposite; he looked as frivolous as Miyano did serious. With his bleached hair and piercings everywhere, he was practically the poster child for juvenile delinquents. Plus he looked sort of mean all the time. Not very approachable. The fact that he was more than 180 cm tall only made him more frightening.

In spite of all that, he always seemed to sound gentle and friendly with Miyano. Very strange. The moment his expression went blank, though, he went right back to looking like a scary upperclassman.

I thought maybe he and Miyano shared a "special" connection—you hear about it all the time at all-boys schools. At the same time, it was just nice to see them being friends. Once, though, I overheard Sasaki talking to Kuresawa, and it made my heart skip a beat.

"I know I'm a little late, but how are your glasses?" Sasaki asked.

"Fine, thanks. The lenses weren't broken. The frame was bent beyond repair, though, so I had to get a new one."

"Scary stuff, huh? I mean, when your eyes are involved."

That was the whole conversation. The reason it stayed with me even though it was so short was the way Kuresawa seemed to get smaller. Almost withering away, as if Sasaki overwhelmed him. Kuresawa was usually completely self-possessed, so I was startled to see him like that. The conversation itself was sort of unsettling, too. It combined to create a negative impression that stayed with me.

Does this mean Sasaki is the reason Kuresawa got hurt? I wondered. "Hmm..." The question bugged me, but I couldn't exactly ask.

From that day forth, I felt vaguely angry at Sasaki. If he was the one who hurt Kuresawa, then maybe Miyano was being forced to hang out with him. Maybe my friend secretly wished he could get away from the guy.

It was Friday, the weekend five of us classmates were going to get cake together, and I was running down the hall. I'd been changing in my classroom when I saw a message on my phone. It was from Kuresawa, and it simply said: Notebook.

"Crap!" I'd shouted. Thankfully, one of the upperclassmen

heard me and let me off the hook for the start of our get-together. I told Hanzawa that I was going to go grab my notebook and water bottle and hurried back to the classroom. We were supposed to turn our notebooks in by today after class, but Kuresawa, the guy responsible for collecting them from us, had asked us to give them to him by noon. Class was already over, and if I didn't catch him, I was finished.

I flung the door open and shouted, "Is Kuresawa still here?!"

"Yeah, barely," he said, looking at his phone and not sounding very impressed. He didn't even glance at me, but I thought I could almost see a halo shining around his head.

"I'm so sorry! Please hand in my notebook for me..." I pulled it out of my desk and handed it to Kuresawa, sighing with relief. He'd sworn vengeance against any of us who didn't hand our stuff in on time, but he didn't look like he was going to run me through right there. He was nice that way.

Miyano was in the room too, although he didn't look like he had any reason to still be there. I thought maybe he was waiting for Kuresawa, but evidently he was on after-class duty and was busy getting the daily report together.

It's just the two of them...

I guess it would have been rude to call this my chance, but I didn't think there was going to be a better time to ask what was on my mind. My curiosity led me to finally break my silence about the relationship between Sasaki and Miyano. Were there feelings involved? Or was Miyano actually cornered?

"Say, Miyano," I said, "I've been wanting to ask you. Are you going out with that upperclassman who's always coming around?"

"What in the world would make you think that?!"

"'Cause this is an all-boys school? And that guy is constantly calling you cute. Huh... So he's just using you?"

"You've got it all wrong!"

After a lengthy discussion, I learned that my assumptions had been just that—assumptions. Totally baseless. In fact, Sasaki was the one who had saved Kuresawa from a violent attack. He was practically a hero. Sasaki and Miyano were just good friends.

Now I feel bad for doubting him, I thought. I left the classroom ruminating on this reminder that "to assume only makes an ass of you and me."

I went along nice and slow, not running, but as I reached the gym, I realized I'd forgotten something important. I was still empty-handed. "Whoopsie! Forgot my water bottle!" I said in a soft singsong tone, and headed back to the classroom. Miyano had already locked up, and I had to go to the faculty office to get the key.

Huh...?

When I got back to the classroom, though, I found the door ajar. That was weird. I was sure it had been closed earlier. I peeked in and saw two figures. One of them was Miyano, but the other wasn't Kuresawa. It was the notorious Sasaki.

Well, I guess he's not really notorious. It turned out he was helping. I had to make sure I remembered that. I backed off a little. This didn't look like a moment when someone should be butting in.

They were talking, but their voices didn't carry to the hallway. Miyano's face was hidden behind the daily report. Sasaki, meanwhile, was stretched out lazily over the desk where Miyano had been writing. I couldn't get a good look at the situation from where I was.

The heck is going on?

I worried that they were having a fight or something. I took a step forward again, but I still couldn't bring myself to enter the room. Miyano and Kuresawa had insisted that Sasaki was a stand-up guy, but I still hadn't quite gotten over the feeling that he seemed a little scary. If it looked like anything was about to happen, I would scream. That would be my plan. If Miyano was in trouble, I had to help him. I was ready.

Silhouetted against the light from the window, I could clearly see Sasaki reach toward Miyano as if he were about to touch him—then draw back without doing anything. Miyano couldn't see it because of the daily report. He probably didn't know it had happened. But I was sure.

Just now, that was...

I swallowed slowly, heavily. Their conversation began to drift to me in snatches. Miyano was speaking unreservedly about what seemed to be the manga he was interested in. Sasaki didn't look like much of a reader. Maybe he was just humoring Miyano.

"Y'know, I saw an ad for something I think was a BL manga at the convenience store today," Sasaki was saying. "Do you know it, Miyaaa?"

"What was the title? Do you remember any of it?"

"Uh, yeah... Wonder if I could search for it. Oh, here it is."

"Oh, this one. It's almost BL but not quite."

Huh? He wasn't scared of Sasaki? Wait... That almost-touch Sasaki gave him, could that have been—?

I was starting to think I could see what was going on between Sasaki and Miyano, and with that, I resolved to stop asking questions. If Miyano was okay with it, that was all I needed to know. *What a load off my chest,* I thought, feeling almost physically lighter. I practically skipped back to the gym, where I announced, "I'm back! I turned my notebook in on time!"

Hanzawa, who seemed to be taking a quick break, said hi to me and then added, "Where's your water bottle?"

"Oh crap!" I looked at the ceiling, realizing I'd forgotten all about it. I definitely didn't want to go back to that classroom, though. Too embarrassing!

INTERLUDE **WHERE THE CALICO DRAWS THE LINE.**

My first year of high school. My first end-of-term since my high school career had started.

I was tired of being a student. Yes, I knew study was essential. But it was just so *boring*. I couldn't muster any desire to actually do it, and I had no idea what I wanted to do with my life.

I wonder how I'm supposed to find something that gives life meaning.

The days were empty and frustrating, yet I knew I would never have them back, and I was fighting it all as hard as I could.

At that time, I—Shuumei Sasaki—hadn't yet found my treasure.

✳✳✳

"This sucks," I mumbled, looking in the mirror one morning. The color in my hair was still patchy. Talk about depressing...

After helping my parents with morning prep at the family bakery, I went back to our house and put on my school uniform, grumbling all the while. My older sister stuck her head into the hallway, and she didn't hesitate to laugh at me as I stood there sighing at the mirror on the shoe rack. That only made me feel worse, but I restrained myself to an annoyed *tsk*.

"How many times have you looked in the mirror since yesterday?" she asked. She'd laughed up a storm the night before too, but I guess she still hadn't had her fill. Maybe it's just amusing to see her little brother freaking out over something like this.

"I wasn't counting," I snarled. In the mirror, my hair was a mess of black patches, sickly brown areas, and rust-colored streaks. Not exactly a natural look. Clearly, I had been wrong to try to use the black hair dye by myself. One of my sister's taunts last night had been that I looked "*like a calico cat.*" It drove me up the wall.

I'd drawn the teachers' ire pretty much right away first term. Partly for my bad attitude, but they also wouldn't shut up about my lightened hair. I knew the inspections were only going to get stricter at the end of the term, and I got so fed up with it that I'd decided to dye my hair black before the closing ceremony.

I wished I could skip school, and I wished I didn't have to take any tests. What was there to look forward to? The minute finals were over, we had the closing ceremony, and you had to take a test *there*, too. They said it wouldn't affect your grades—that they were only going to use it as a reference for remedial summer guidance—but then why take it at all? Just thinking about it made my head spin. Admittedly, I was the one who'd applied to a program with lots of supplementary lectures, so as much as I really did want to get away from it all, I also had the urge to stick it out.

Even without all that other stuff, though, I still would have been pretty ticked about the hair-dye situation. It wasn't just my sister—everyone at school was gonna laugh at me. I could live with that, but it meant other students I normally never spoke to would be paying attention to me. The thought alone made me feel a little sick.

"I can't believe this…"

"Grit your teeth and bear it. Maybe it'll teach you not to treat everything like a huge pain in the neck."

"Sucks…"

"You're hopeless!"

She didn't have to tell me. I knew it was a bad habit. I was the one who had to live with it! I went with the flow to avoid anything that might involve effort or trouble, but I was the one who paid for it in the end. I already knew from my experience in middle school where it would lead: After things got worse and worse because I wasn't doing anything about my situation, I would end up stuck somewhere I wasn't happy about.

I'd like to think I was already a little better than that. At least I was going to school pretty regularly now, not like then. I had a tendency to skip class, sure, but I didn't feel like I was throwing away my studies in the same way. Take today: I was so bent on making the end-of-term a success that I had even tried to dye my hair.

I knew perfectly well that from the outside, I didn't exactly look like a model student. I knew I hadn't made any huge, dramatic leaps. It still all seemed like a lot of trouble to me, but I thought I was all right for now. *Just gotta give it my best shot…*

I picked up the schoolbag I'd tossed by the front door and shoved my feet into my sneakers.

"Did you get any bread?" my sister asked.

"Don't need it. We've only got morning classes today. I'll eat somewhere."

"Okay, have a nice day."

"...Thanks."

The bakery opened so early that my family was rarely around to see me off in the morning. Even my sister hadn't said a proper good-bye in a long time. It felt strange. I gave a quick nod to hide my embarrassment. As I went out the door, the summer sun assaulted my eyes. After just a few steps, I already felt like the heat was clinging to my skin and weighing me down, almost as if it was out to sap my motivation.

At school, the reaction was every bit as obnoxious as I'd expected. It started with Ogasawara remarking, "Back to black, eh? Been a while." He was bringing up stuff from our first couple years of middle school! Talk about a pain in the ass. And what about *his* hair? He had streaks in it! He wasn't even *trying* to follow the dress code. I should've told him where he could shove his "back to black."

I wasn't surprised when he got stopped by the Disciplinary Committee's inspectors and called out in homeroom. As for me, they stopped me on account of my patchy look, but I was exonerated by the fact that I'd been trying to dye my hair black and wasn't penalized. They did give me a little grief about my lax posture, though.

What about Hirano? He had bleached hair, but he served on the Disciplinary Committee. I guess he got away with it because otherwise he was pretty by-the-book about school

138

rules. In other words, I could draw the line where I felt like it. It wouldn't make sense to try to change everything at once. Ask too much of myself, and I'd never make it.

The first thing Ogasawara did when he came over to my house wasn't apologize. It was to say, "Hey, color's back," staring hard at my hair. After my disastrous first attempt at dyeing it, I'd finally gotten it looking neat again on the second try. I'd used up a bunch of my sister's hair treatment trying not to damage my locks doing all this dyeing. So far, she hadn't found out.

"Yeah. And I'm never dyeing it again," I said, grumbling about how much work it had been.

Ogasawara grinned. "You're gonna spend a lot of time at school after classes."

He was right. The penalty for dyeing your hair was to stay late for a lecture, but that was all. Just a bit of "guidance" where they browbeat you about not letting your standards slip just because it was almost summer break.

When Ogasawara and my other friends told me, I almost couldn't believe my ears. *All that...for what?*

"It'd be worth it!" I said with a big sigh as Ogasawara started rifling through my CD collection.

CHAPTER
8 LAID-BACK & TROUBLE.

It was in May of my first year of high school that I, Taiga Hirano, encountered the "hooky monster," Sasaki. It started with a conversation we shared in a part of the school students weren't supposed to be in. After that, a whole year passed, and we never got especially close. The next year, when we had underclassmen of our own to look out for, I would see a completely new side of Sasaki. But at the beginning, I couldn't imagine it.

✳✳✳

I was putting a handout about an intensive math course in a clear folder and wondering whether I should apply to take it. It had been a bit over a month since school started, and having grown accustomed to dorm life, I was starting to think about how to tackle the tests I would eventually have to take. This math class was aimed at kids in the advanced program, but in principle, anyone could participate.

I couldn't tell whether it would be a good fit for me. I had been thinking about going home that weekend; in fact, I'd just called my family about it. I was a little embarrassed to go right back home after I'd just gotten back from Golden Week vacation. I guess it showed that I was pretty homesick. But the upperclassman I was living with warned me that if I didn't go home again until summer break, my parents would worry about me, and I thought that made sense. Still, I hesitated.

My visit wouldn't be happening for a couple weeks yet, so I could still change my mind. I didn't like that idea, though, since my parents had adjusted their own schedules to accommodate me. I might just be a high schooler, but living in the dorm had given me an idea of all the trouble involved when you had to make changes to a routine schedule.

I'm still sort of feeling my way along, though. At the moment, the scales were tilting toward focusing on subjects I felt fairly comfortable in and putting off the rest. Oh well. I had time. I could use the midterm exams to help me make my decision. And since I had all week to decide, maybe I could consult with the other guys in the dorm for a while. I sat there thinking about it so long that before I knew it, I was one of only a few people left in the classroom.

"Why didn't you answer the phone yesterday, man? I was at the end of my rope!"

This explosive accusation came from Ogasawara, a guy with a streak dyed right down the middle of his hair that gave him a tough-guy edge. You would never have taken him for a first-year. He had some piercings too, but so did I. I couldn't exactly criticize him for it.

"Yesterday? I had work," Sasaki replied lazily. His hair was, well, less distinctive, but he had so many piercings, it was pain-ful to look at. I didn't think many students had several holes through their cartilage. I wasn't about to judge a guy by his looks, but Sasaki was unusual. He stood out in our class, where devotion to study was expected.

"Don't lie to me! I saw your sister yesterday, and she said you were asleep in your room!"

"Was I? I guess."

Talk about laid-back! He was way too indifferent! Yet Sasaki sounded so totally free of malice that it made Ogasawara seem like the bad guy just for trying to get him to tell the truth.

"Hey, what about that CD we talked about the other day?" Ogasawara said.

"Oh, that. Forgot it."

What are they, a comedy duo?

"Grr!"

I listened silently to the banter between the apathetic Sasaki and straightforward Ogasawara. I was just starting to stand when I remembered: Sasaki had good grades in math. I was pretty sure he'd gotten the top score on the midterm exams. That was where I'd gotten the notion that he had a serious side, even if he didn't look like it.

What a carefree guy.

That was my first impression of Shuumei Sasaki.

My second impression was different.

"Class leader!" called the Modern Lit teacher, poking his head into our room.

"He's not here today, sir," someone called back.

"Someone from the Disciplinary Committee, then!"

That would be me.

"Yes, sir?" I said. There were no classes today and nothing to hand in this week. What did he want with me?

"Sasaki's the only person who didn't hand in last week's worksheet. I told him to have it to me by yesterday, but I haven't seen hide nor hair of him. Tell him to get it to me *today*, will you?"

This was considered Disciplinary Committee business?

"Er... All right, sir," I said, nodding and resisting the urge to ask why this wasn't the after-class duty students' responsibility.

Ugh, why'd I have to get dragged into this? I managed not to grumble out loud as I looked around the classroom. Of course, there was no sign of Sasaki. Still, I was sure I'd seen him that morning, and his bag was at his desk.

"You know where Sasaki is today?" I asked Ogasawara. I saw them together a lot; maybe he would know. But he shook his head.

"No idea."

"I don't have his contact info. Don't have my phone, either," I said.

"It's cool, just a moment. I'll give him a ring," Ogasawara replied. "...Hey, Sasaki? Where are you right now? Huh? What do you mean, you're *up*? Hey!" The other end of the line went silent. It was nice of Ogasawara to save me the trouble of calling, but Sasaki had evidently wasted it. Not that I understood why or what was going on.

"What's the deal?" I asked.

"He hung up on me. If I had to guess, I'd say he's probably napping somewhere because it's hot today." Ogasawara looked pretty upset, but for the first time, it occurred to me that maybe he was just making a scary face and wasn't actually angry.

There was no hint of annoyance in his voice. In fact, he was a far cry from me—I was feeling pretty pissed.

"Well, where is he?" I demanded, but Ogasawara just scratched his head and made a noncommittal sound. I could tell he wasn't trying to put me off; he really didn't know.

"He hates the heat, so he's probably somewhere cool," he said. This guy was unbelievable. Not Ogasawara. I meant Sasaki.

The bell for fourth period rang a moment later, but Sasaki was still a no-show.

Can't believe he skipped morning classes. Why does he even bother coming to school? Did *he even come to school today?*

I tried to hide my annoyance the whole way through lunch. The lunch boxes you could order at school were never enough for me on days when I had gym class, and I was feeling particularly unsatisfied today. It didn't help that I had eaten way quicker than usual, thinking I would use the lunch break to find Sasaki. I'd searched everywhere I thought someone might go to play hooky: the benches in the courtyard, the arts-and-music-type classrooms along infrequently-traveled hallways. I worked my way from floor to floor up the school, looking everywhere I could think of.

There were surprisingly few rooms that went completely unused. Almost everywhere I thought to look, I discovered someone having lunch. Before long, I found myself out of ideas. What was this, a game of hide-and-seek?

There was only one place I hadn't checked—the school roof. But that was supposed to be off-limits to students. The Astronomy Club was allowed up there occasionally to look at the sky, but even that was just a few times a year. They hadn't even done it since I'd started school here.

I'm pretty sure the roof is locked... Right? With nothing but my suspicions to go on, I looked up the stairs to the roof. *Ogasawara said Sasaki hates the heat.* From that perspective, the stairway to the roof looked like a cozy hole in the ground.

I pushed aside the whiteboard proclaiming that the roof was for "authorized personnel only" and took a hesitant step onto the stairs. I worked my way up to the landing, doing my damnedest not to make a sound. I turned and saw someone.

"*There* you are!" I sighed.

Sasaki was at the uppermost part of the staircase. The door to the roof was indeed locked, and the only window that let any light in was far away. Sasaki was sitting in a shadowy spot, leaning against the cool wall, listening to music.

"Oh," he said, his eyes drifting open. His *ya-caught-me* expression seemed out of place on the dusty staircase. It was the disinterested reaction of a guy who just didn't care about school.

"The hell are you doing here?" I said. Had he really been sitting there all day? Didn't his butt get sore?

Sasaki slid off his headphones and gave me a questioning look. "Er, Hirano, right? Whatcha need?"

He remembers my name? That surprised me. Maybe my golden hair gave it away.

"What do I need? To tell you that you have to turn in a worksheet for Modern Literature today. You're the only one who hasn't."

Only then did it occur to me that it would have been far more efficient just to have Ogasawara send him a text. I'd been asked to *tell* him to turn in the worksheet, but I wasn't ordered to collect it from him. Still, it was true that I was concerned

about his "flying by the seat of his pants" approach to life. Maybe we were *supposed* to be having this conversation.

"Oh, that. Didn't do it."

"Do you have it with you?"

Modern Literature wasn't on the schedule today, so I didn't expect much—but to my surprise, Sasaki nodded. "I think it's in my bag." Small blessings. This particular worksheet didn't draw directly from the textbook, so as long as you had the handout, you could manage.

"Okay. Well, if you get back there and work on it right now, you can probably hand it in after class. If there's anything you don't understand, you can ask me."

"You the class rep, Hirano? I forget."

For a second, I thought maybe he was being snarky, but it seemed to be an earnest question. "Disciplinary Committee," I said. "Hey, speaking of which, you're not supposed to be up here."

"But it's nice and cool."

His answers never gave me anything to work with, and I was getting tired of it. He didn't have any malice; he just didn't have any motivation, either. It felt pointless talking to him. I was getting annoyed. "You need to cool off, go to the nurse's office. Isn't it pretty chilly there?"

"Yeah, but there'd be upperclassmen. How'm I supposed to relax like that?"

So he had a timid side. I'd never thought Sasaki would be the kind to care if there were older guys around.

"You're being delinquent, but that's a problem? Make it make sense," I said.

He pointedly looked away from me. "I'm not a delinquent anymore. Anyway, delinquents are supposed to fight, and I don't like fighting. I'm not any good at it." I almost would have said he was pouting, and somewhere behind the brazen exterior I realized there was a certain childishness. *He doesn't really fit in here, does he?*

"Hey," I said, "why'd you pick this school? They expect you to study hard here. If you play hooky all the time, you'll get left behind."

He could probably continue to keep his head above water in his best subjects; a baseline level of academic ability would buy him a few months before his grades started to drop. Life would be a lot harder, though, in other subjects—ones he didn't suck at but didn't excel at, either. The advanced course, which we belonged to, started off in first-year with lectures aimed at getting you ready to take college entrance exams. There were supplementary lectures on a regular basis, extra classes that were supposedly optional but which were pretty much obligatory. Someone skipping several times a week like Sasaki would soon find it hard to keep up even in the remedial lectures.

I was sure he'd heard all that pretty much since he got here…but maybe he hadn't been listening.

"Oh, that… I was told to go to the best school I could get into," he said with more than a hint of self-deprecation. "What about you, Hirano?"

He seemed to mean that he'd come to this school to satisfy his parents or maybe his teachers. If I thought that should have affronted his sense of personal initiative, well, his estimation of himself was too low for that. It was enough if he could do his bit with the direction he'd been pointed in. You completed the high school general-education curriculum before you had to decide what you were going to do with your future, so he would have plenty of opportunities to make his own choices later.

"Me? There's something I want to do, and I thought this school could help me do it."

"So you thought hard about this stuff, huh? Nice. That's nice." The look on his face, a gentle expression tinged with envy, seemed impossibly sad. I glared at him. It was too soon for him to sit aloof from his classmates, avoiding effort, resigned to his fate. It was still only May. May of our first year! I couldn't stand here and watch one of our classmates drop out of his own life.

"You find something, too," I said.

"Huh?"

I took a deep breath, and, taking care not to let myself start shouting, I said, "You picked the best school you could swing. Well, now you're here. So find *something*. I don't care if it's a reason not to be late or something you want to do... Er, wait, should that be '*make the effort to find something*'?" I wasn't used to this whole lecturing thing.

Sasaki chuckled. "Wish I could. Hey, you're even more of a delinquent than I am, Hirano."

I hadn't expected that remark, and it touched a nerve. *Hey, he's awfully cheeky for someone I've just met.*

"What do you mean? I show up to class every day."

"That hair color. Isn't that against school rules?"

"It's okay. I make sure my uniform is up to standard."

It was true. I never let my uniform look sloppy, and I wore the mandated color of shirt under my uniform jacket even on days when there were no inspections.

"So you can, but I can't?"

"The point is, I show I *can* follow school rules when I need to. So who cares what I do with my hair? It doesn't have anything to do with my grades anyway."

"I think I'm starting to get it," Sasaki said. He wrapped his arms around himself and then yawned widely.

He wants *to pull himself up*, I thought. *He just hasn't found anything to give him that push.*

Not that it was any business of mine.

"Sun's pretty high in the sky by now. There shouldn't be any direct sunlight on your desk this time of day," I said. "You came all the way to school. As long as you have the chance to make the effort, why not make it?"

With that encouragement, Sasaki got to his feet, swaying slightly. As I watched him brush the dust off his uniform, I decided to suggest to the Disciplinary Committee that we should make sure this area got swept periodically. We wouldn't want any part of the school, even one off-limits to students, to look grimy.

"Mmm... Well, I guess I could handle one worksheet. If you'll help me, Hirano." The way he still seemed completely harmless was almost funny.

"Yeah, I'll help you. *If* you really have it with you. If you don't, then go talk to the teacher and get another copy before lunch is over."

"Yeah, yeah."

I almost cracked a smile at the sense of friendliness he exuded. "You should only say 'yeah' once. Break's over in five minutes, you know. You could stand to look like you're sweating it a little."

This time, Sasaki drew it out into a single "yeeeah." He started down the stairs, and I fell into step beside him. "Hey, give me your phone number," I said softly, rushing it out.

"You?" he said, apparently not expecting that at all.

I was surprised to discover I felt a rush of embarrassment. I kept my eyes determinedly forward. "It's a pain in the ass not being able to get ahold of you." It felt funny, looking after a guy my own age like this, but I couldn't stop myself. I figured getting Sasaki's contact info now would make it easier if I needed something with him in the future.

Shuumei Sasaki.

My first impression was that he did things by the seat of his pants. My second—that he was a lot of trouble.

"I've got an idea. If you're so averse to heat, then close the curtain when you get here in the morning." Even if he just drew the shades near him to stop the sunlight from heating his own seat, it would have to make him feel cooler.

"Hmm," he said, but he didn't sound very convinced. I was starting to think it would take a while for this guy to find his calling—what he loved to do.

We walked back to the classroom, chatting about whatever. I learned that his family ran a bakery, and that since his third year of middle school, he'd been getting up early in the morning to help prepare for each day. No wonder he always seemed to be eating bread at lunch.

"So you help your family in the mornings? What's the point if it just makes you fall asleep in class?" I said. I knew early mornings must be busy for a bakery, but if it was making Sasaki push himself too hard, then I thought he ought to stop. Easy for me to say as an outsider and a layperson. Maybe he could at least limit himself to helping on weekends, when it wouldn't be a detriment to his school attendance.

"Believe it or not, it's actually a lot of fun," Sasaki said, looking placid as ever. Huh. So it really mattered to him. Even if that wasn't enough by itself.

"If you don't want the school to force you to quit, you'd better at least show up to class so they don't start sniffing around." The teachers and staff already had their eyes on Sasaki.

He looked at the ground. The tardiness in particular was really hurting him. Even on days when he didn't outright skip class, he tended to show up at the last possible second, so the first-hour teachers really had it out for him.

"I will," he said, but he sounded unconcerned about it. At the time, I still didn't sense any passion from him, any serious proactiveness. I thought he was just arbitrarily shrugging off my ideas. Well, it wasn't my job to lecture him into the ground. Once we were done with that worksheet and it was safely turned in, I wouldn't have any reason to keep talking to him.

We went along, classmates but not much more, and in due course, we both moved up a year.

It was more than a year after I met him that Sasaki really started to change—namely, in July of our second year. I never could have predicted the incident that started him on this personal transformation. Nor who it was that got his attention. And I never expected the look I would see on his face.

Special Thanks!

To the writer, Kotoko Hachijo:
You did a great job with the *Hirano and Kagiura* novel, and in this follow-up, you really captured the nuances of these characters and a bunch of great behind-the-scenes details. Thank you for working so hard right until the deadline!

To the editor, Sakurazawa:
Thank you for going over the proofreader's corrections so many times and managing to work so many of my hopes and dreams into this book. I appreciated how I could trust you to make sure all the spelling and lettering was correct, including the handwritten stuff. I know how many times you checked to make sure the glosses on words throughout the book were right. I can only apologize for all the trouble I caused you! I'm sure you also did other things I don't even know about, but I'm grateful for those, too. I had a lot going on at once, including this novel, and it was your prowess at organizing things that kept me from getting overwhelmed. Thank you so much!

To everyone at the Gene Editorial Department who cooperated:
You're all amazing. Thank you for helping me get a second novel out! I'm sure some of the people in this department helped check this book, and they have my thanks! I look forward to working with you again on the next one.

To my assistant Kana Toka:
You helped with drawing backgrounds, thanks to which I was able to submit the manuscript. Thank you very much!

To my assistant my mom:
Thank you for always getting the screentone painted in about an hour before the deadline. Oh, and also for the fact that I exist.

To the designer, Kawatani Design:
This time the front and back covers are different colors; the whole *feel* of the book is something different than usual—but thanks to you, it's still just as sweet and refreshing as ever! With you behind me, I'm always able to draw the covers I want at the size I want them. Thank you!

To everyone at RUHIA Ltd.:
You handled the typesetting for this book as well as the last one. Once again, I was fiddling with the text until the last possible moment, and I know that could have impacted the final product... You worked yourselves to the bone and got this out the door. Thank you so much!

To Daisuke Shinseki (RUHIA Ltd.):
You were in charge of proofreading once again. Thank you for giving the manuscript an incredibly thorough reading, from correcting slips in the first-person pronoun usage to hounding me about parts of the narrative that didn't flow to pointing out how real people tend to relate to their past actions. You gave me so many opportunities to think harder about how the story was constructed.

To everyone in the Sales Department:
I owe you a lot, not just for the last book, but now for this one, too! Thank you for your ideas for bookstore-specific bonuses! Looking forward to working with you on the next one.

Also, the printer, who always comes up with the most beautiful colors; the delivery person, who makes sure everything gets to us safely; all the bookstores; the publishing agency; and everyone else without whom this book wouldn't and couldn't exist. Thank you all so much!

Finally, thank you to everyone on Twitter and Pixiv who read and supported the original manga. Thanks to you, the novel project was a success. And extra-special thanks to those who picked up this book!

So many people gave their time, effort, and ideas to help make this book a reality. Thank you all!

Shou Harusono

2020.3

Afterword.

Nice to meet you! I'm Kotoko Hachijo. This is my second spin-off novel after *Hirano and Kagiura.*

In these stories, I put the spotlight on a variety of characters, from Sasaki and Hirano in their first year to "Miya" and his friends in their first year. I particularly focused on filling out Kuresawa's and Tashiro's stories. It was really exciting to get to expand parts of the "SasaMiya" world that we only get glimpses of in the main work.

There are a lot of scenes that tie this novel to the manga. You might be surprised by what you learn. You might witness the struggles surrounding one particular incident or say to yourself, "So-and-so was there in *that* scene?!" My hope is that this novel will help readers rediscover the pleasures of *Sasaki and Miyano.*

My thanks go out to all the readers who sent their feedback on the *Hirano and Kagiura* novel. I tried to show my gratitude by sending New Year's greeting cards this year to everyone who included an address. (If anyone didn't get theirs, I'm sorry...)

I had so much fun on the last book that it was an honor and a pleasure to get to do another one. So many people helped make this book happen, but in particular I want to thank Harusono and the editor, Sakurazawa. All the "SasaMiya" readers out there have my profound gratitude as well. Thank you all very, very much.

Kotoko Hachijo

Afterword.

Hello! Harusono here. Now we not only have a *Hirano and Kagiura* novel but a *Sasaki and Miyano* one as well! Kotoko Hachijo once again handled the writing duties, and she has my profuse thanks!

Thanks to everyone who picked up the last book, we were able to do a second novel. Thanks to you, the readers, Sasaki and Miyano's world is growing. Thank you so much.

Unlike the last novel, this one is written in first person. Despite being a collection of short stories from a variety of perspectives, it should still be easy to follow. If it is, you can thank Hachijo for her tireless work in making it that way. I certainly do!

This novel focuses on the first year of high school, which mostly occurred in the gap between Volumes 1 and 2 of the manga. Each time I introduced a new character, I tried to think hard enough about who they were and where they came from that I could have done a thirty-page short story about them. But because those stories weren't relevant to the main relationship between Sasaki and Miyano, I never included them. Well, here they are—in novel form!

Let me highlight some things I liked in this book.

For the opening of the Kuresawa story, I had this vague idea that I wanted a sort of "start of a romance" thing. When I saw what Hachijo came up with—"It marked the beginning of my new life with her"—I was like, "Now, *that's* being young in a nutshell!!!!!" The whole world seemed to sparkle.

Then there's the end of chapter 3: "Maybe he'd stumbled on someone who would be a good influence on him." It made my heart race, like, "Could Hirano possibly say that?!" Hachijo has a gift for these lines that end on the perfect note and just sort of stay with you. After I read them, I would close my eyes and soak in them, like a bath.

Personally, I have a special soft spot for Tashiro's first-person pronoun (he uses *ore*, a strongly masculine pronoun in Japanese). It shows how he's got that edge buried under his kindness and decency. One of the bookstore bonuses Hachijo wrote was about what was happening with him before the cultural festival, and I really appreciated it!

Hachijo seems to have read the manga extremely carefully. (That's my assumption, anyway, and I'm not questioning it!) For example, after Kuresawa gets in that fight, she mentions how the lenses of his glasses weren't broken. There's a single panel of his flashback in Volume 3 that shows him holding his glasses with the lenses intact, and I have to think that's where she got the idea from. It was in the manga, but it wasn't necessarily in my description of the character, yet she picked up on it anyway. I'm really impressed and grateful.

She also took care to give expression to some shifts of feeling that were sort of vague in the manga, stuff where, plot-wise, I was like, "Ehh... More or less like this." (Even in the manga, there were things I kept changing right to the bitter end.) Over and over again, I found myself nodding along, like, "Ohhh! Yes! Yes! That! That's exactly how it happened!"

What I'm saying is, I had lots of fun supervising the novel as it took shape. I hope you'll enjoy it alongside the manga version.

If you have a chance, please do send your thoughts and feedback!

To: Kotoko Hachijo and/or Shou Harusono
Attn: Gene Pixiv Editorial Department
Kadokawa Corporation
2-13-12 Fujimi, Chiyoda-ku, Tokyo 102-8177, Japan

2020. 3.
Shou Harusono

Sasaki and Miyano

The Japanese
edition of this novel
includes bonus manga.
Flip to the back of the
book, read right to
left, and enjoy!

AN UPPERCLASSMAN MATTERS

A CHERISHED UNDERCLASSMAN

END

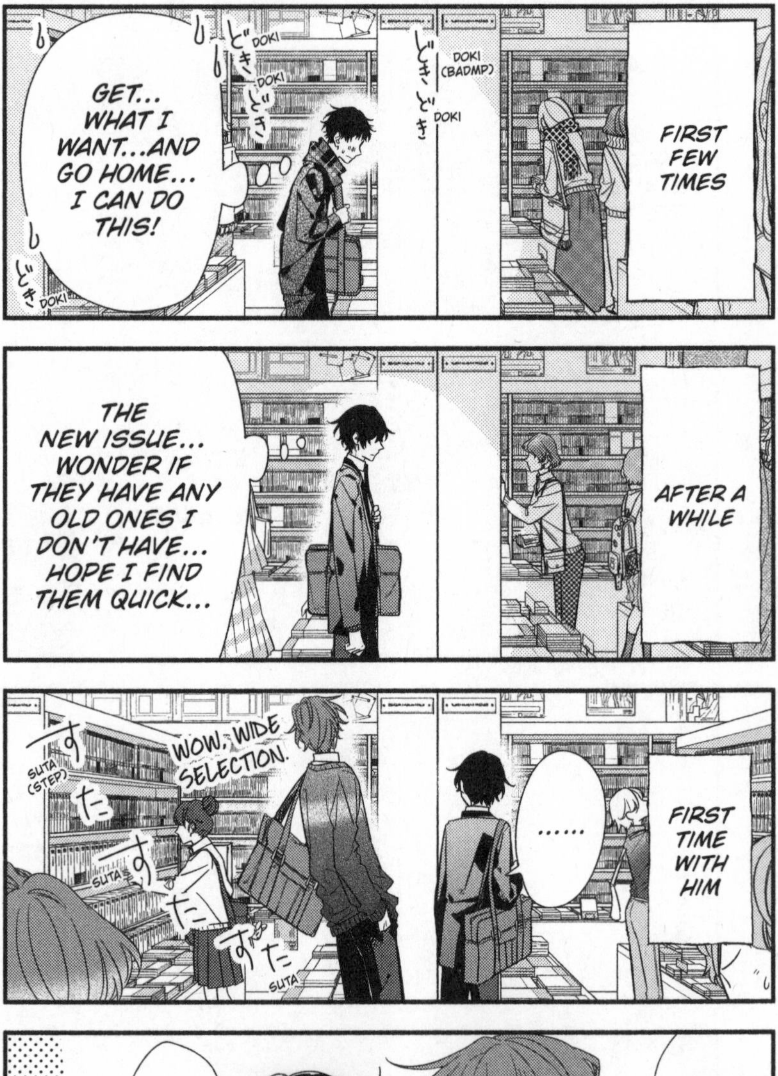

LUMPED TOGETHER.

YOU LIKE THIS ONE?

CUTE BOTTOM: IDOL

I'LL PAY.

IT'S FINE...

GOTTA DO THESE THINGS RIGHT.

YEAH, I LIKE IT. THANKS.

WHAT ABOUT THIS ONE?

GUESS THIS IS MY KIND'A THING...

UH, SURE...

HUH? IT'S ALMOST LIKE...

I JUST WANT A QUIET SCHOOL LIFE! STUDENT X IDOL X COMPANY PREZ'S LOVERS!?
TOP: ELIGIBLE PRESIDENT!
BOTTOM: ENTHUSIASTIC IDOL!

AND THIS ONE?

BESPECTACLED PERFECTIONIST SADO-MANAGER

×

A DARK-HAIRED IDOL WITH A PAST!

GLOOMY IDOL-OTAKU CHILDHOOD FRIEND

"I WANT TO QUIT BEING AN IDOL..."

YUU-CHAN... IT'S OKAY TO QUIT BEING AN IDOL.

"WHY'D YOU BECOME AN IDOL?"

"EVER SINCE YOU TIED ME UP, YUI-CHAN..."

...GETTING MORE AND MORE ACCURATE!

HE'S GOT MY FETISH NAILED DOWN!

YES! I LIKE IT A LOT.

HE'S...

PHEW!

A BOYFRIEND WHO LEARNS QUICKLY.